Praise for Anne Dunlop

On *The Pineapple Tart*

"This book is sheer bliss."
The Sunday World

"Funny, tender-hearted, immensely satisfying."
Woman's Way

On *A Soft Touch*

"A gloriously entertaining tale . . . it's a definite must."
The Sunday World

On *The Dolly Holiday*

"Her following will grow immensely with this novel."
Woman's Way

"Quirky and humorous."
Cork Examiner

kissing the frog

kissing the frog

ANNE DUNLOP

POOLBEG

Published 1996
by Poolbeg Press Ltd
123 Baldoyle Industrial Estate
Dublin 13, Ireland

The Publishers gratefully acknowledge the support of The Northern
Ireland Arts Council.

A catalogue record for this book is available from the British Library.

ISBN 1 85371 440 2

Cover photography by Attard Photolibrary, London
Cover design by Poolbeg Group Services Ltd
Set by Poolbeg Group Services Ltd in Goudy 11.5/14.5
Printed by The Guernsey Press Ltd,
Vale, Guernsey, Channel Islands.

About the Author

Anne Dunlop was born in Castledawson, Co Derry, Northern Ireland in 1968. She graduated in Agricultural Science at UCD. Anne Dunlop now works as an air stewardess for Gulf Air. This is her fourth novel for Poolbeg.

Also by Anne Dunlop

The Pineapple Tart
A Soft Touch
The Dolly Holiday

Published by Poolbeg

For Carol Percy

part one

chapter one

I remember spitting gravel and picking hockey pitch from between my teeth. And Ms Dart yelling "Jolly hockey sticks, Sonia, another marvellous goal," as the final whistle blew. My sickening friend had scored three goals already. "You've played your heart out, Sonia."

I'd been offside four times and, with a bit of luck, might have been dropped from the school team. As Ms Dart delighted in reminding me, there were a hundred pairs of hockey-playing legs in the school just waiting to take my place. She always gave the impression that she was resisting the urge to sink her toe into my fat and dimpled bottom. I often wished I had the nerve to tell her to stick her hockey ball where the sun don't shine. Boring, boring hockey casting shadows over every Saturday of my adolescence. Now I'm twenty-eight I wonder why I just didn't chuck the team and go to Scripture Union instead.

But I never did. You were only a rebel at my school if you weren't clever enough to conform, and it was a social disgrace to be dropped from the school team. People would have talked about me, pointed at me in the corridor, sniggered in the school toilets.

Far better to be like Sonia whose hockey skirt blew off when she swung for the final goal and everyone saw the lovebite she got on her bum on Thursday night at the rugby disco.

My mother had taken us and the rugby boys on the door said, "Sonia Anderson can't be your friend, Big Marian, she's too good-looking."

It was a typical rugby-playing conversation opener but it did nothing for my self-confidence and I may have sat with a face while Sonia danced off with Jimmy Fingers who was physically gross and who danced with every girl until he got one to take him.

Paddy Butler, "a fine thing but don't tell him," asked me to go outside with him during the slow set but I didn't fancy Paddy because he was a Catholic and I wasn't allowed to. Instead of being mature about it, I got really flustered and said, "What sort of girl do you take me for, Paddy?" and he'd shrugged and taken Sonia outside instead.

Jimmy Fingers finally got to the bottom of the barrel and blew half-heartedly into my hair to judge if I was desperate as he was, so I hit him over the head with my handbag. Fingers, an animal and an active member of Derryrose Young Farmers' Club, pulled my pop-on shoes off and threw them around the disco floor.

Sonia hadn't stopped telling people about the lovebite since it happened. She cornered Mr Sterling during

Friday's rat dissection and pulled her skirt up and thrust her buttock into his face, but he refused to be impressed. "I swear that rat was dead when I gave it to you," he said. And in the showers after the match, while we admired the teeth marks, she told us she was never going to a rugby disco again because the flashing lights had made her dizzy and she'd tripped over one of my pop-on shoes, and everyone said she was drunk.

Call me old-fashioned, but I couldn't stomach communal showers and the endless parade of pubescent tits and bums. So while Sonia, possessor of a very pert set, demonstrated how she could jump into her panties I discreetly removed my hockey knickers beneath a towel. Then I slipped out of the changing rooms with my hood up so Ms Dart wouldn't be able to see me and frogmarch me back and personally supervise my personal hygiene.

I was hoping I wouldn't see Paddy Butler on the rugby pitch either. Since I'd been propositioned on Thursday night, I hadn't been able to look him in the face. Paddy's eyes undressed me and made me feel uncomfortable.

He wrote an essay once, for the school magazine, about the Advantages of Smoking and how you could pick up strange girls in discos by asking them if they had a light. The way to inject life into a flagging chat-up was to offer the object of your admiration a cigarette. He laughed and laughed when I said, "None of my friends smoke, Paddy."

So he'd known that the "cigarette" approach wouldn't work on Thursday night but the direct approach hadn't worked either.

3

Of course his essay didn't get published, nor did his poems, Ode To a Toilet and one about different ways to kill yourself. Instead my poem about capital punishment was chosen, and the piece about Sonia's French exchange trip was tastefully edited to half a page and a photograph of Notre Dame. Sonia complained for days that they'd interfered with her artistic integrity by cutting out all the sexual innuendoes and bad words she knew in French.

I was in a hot fantasy by the time I was passing the rugby pitches. I had several fantasies at seventeen that I took out and played with. It was quite a harmless hobby, but I was always afraid to tell anyone in case the men in white coats were sent for, to take me away.

In my fantasy it was me, not Sonia, who'd scored the last magnificent goal. Half backs had been known to score goals. I even scored one by accident once. Actually I kicked it in past the goalie in one of those dogfights you get in the circle of under-fourteen hockey. Fist and fur was flying so nobody noticed my fancy footwork and I never let on. Usually I didn't tell lies, even in my fantasies. When someone tells a lie the angels cry. Ms Dart yelled, "Jolly marvellous goal, Marian," something I couldn't imagine her saying in thumbscrews.

In my fantasy the entire First XV were jogging past to warm up for their own game and witnessed the brilliant goal and Ms Dart's congratulations. And one of the rugby boys (any one of them provided he was Protestant, I wasn't fussy) was so impressed he asked me to be his guest at the Wednesday cup matches – Sonia was a brilliant hockey player and she was always being asked to cup matches; there was a seat on the rugby bus with her name on it.

There was a pile of wolf whistling coming from the rugby pitches but I didn't look round. I was too afraid it was the rugby boys making fun of me. I'd turn round and they'd all laugh and say, "You didn't think we were wolf whistling at you, did you, Big Marian?"

Adolescent boys can be so cruel and what's more frightening is that the majority of them grow up and never change. Look at the average rugby-playing bum and consider the average rugby-playing brain. But I would still have given my right arm to be "Guest of A Rugby Boy" once in my life. It was my *Jim'll Fix It* ambition at seventeen.

It was actually Sonia wolf whistling with two fingers from the window of the white Vauxhall Nova she shared with her mother. When Sonia passed her driving test, her parents offered her the family Mini, but Sonia stamped her little foot and said she wouldn't be seen dead in a Mini, so Mrs Anderson bought a Vauxhall Nova and they made the Mini into a hen-house.

The Andersons have a huge dairy farm outside Magherafelt and Sonia was a superb hockey player because she practised in a cleaned-out slurry pit. Santa brought her a new hockey stick every Christmas.

When she first played for Ireland internationally, in Germany, the entire Anderson family drove to Dublin to pick her up from the plane. You'd have thought there was no transport between North and South.

Sonia was always getting wolf whistles. She frequently went up the street after skills' practice in her hockey skirt and got wolf whistled. Then she'd giggle and say her reputation was ruined.

"You're nothing but a slut," I told her, but secretly and shamefully I wished I could have the opportunity to have mine ruined too.

Naughty and lascivious thoughts often popped into my "white as the driven snow" mind at seventeen. I wonder, do they crowd the minds of all young virgins? It was not a discussion I would have considered initiating. For I had a Christian Conscience. I used to imagine the CC as an angel dressed in a white sheet playing a harp and crying when I upset it. Now I reckon it was a shriekingly middle-class spinster-like spoilsport, with a sharp nose. Heavily religious without a shred of godliness or sympathy.

Boy, could my Christian Conscience bitch. To think naughty thoughts, even if they did slip unbidden into my head, was as bad as doing them, it told me. I was apparently harbouring the intent in my heart.

And I shouldn't have been playing hockey, when I could have been going to Scripture Union.

And I shouldn't have been going to rugby discos. It was a backsliding attitude to say I was "witnessing" by going and not drinking and not going outside with Paddy Butler. Some other Christian with weaker flesh (and more offers), might have got led into bad ways. It would have been my fault for leading by example. There is no "Do as I say, not as I do" with one's Christian Conscience.

What a conscience-stricken, guilt-ridden, inferiority-complexed little prig I was. Angst-ridden. Still too young to laugh at myself. Growing up, like hockey, was a game I was no good at. I kept my eyes on my watch then too, wondering how much longer it was going to last.

And wishing, fatly, that I was popular at church parties. But all the games needed partners and I was never picked. It was hideously depressing because I didn't know what I was doing wrong. My mother advised me to smile more ("Smile though your heart is breaking, Marian"). Sonia said I should just have homed in on the boys I wanted like she did, and not wait to be asked. In the end I chose to be a wallflower in a dimly-lit discotheque. The person who bottles popularity will make a fortune.

Sonia wasn't behind the door when popularity was being handed out. I stood in her shadow, and tried to bask gratefully in her reflected glory.

"Get into my car," said Sonia. "I've a pile of magazines here for you."

She tooted the horn a couple of times so everyone could see her. "Get in, Marian, before the country sees you in that terrible twenty-eight-inch skirt."

She wanted to talk about Paddy Butler of the LoveBite on the Bum scandal. She thought she fancied him. Nothing new. Sonia had fancied a hundred different rugby boys a hundred times before. She was obsessed with them and her personality changed when she came within half a mile of a rugby ball. Sonia wasn't any better-looking than me, but she still got to all the rugby matches as Guest of a Rugby Boy.

"At the Wednesday cup match he swallowed a bottle of *Black Bush* on the way home and was drunk for a hour before passing out. He fell asleep on my shoulder. I slept a bit too. I was exhausted. I'd been up half the night drying my baseball boots with a hairdryer. Paddy put his arm around me and said there was a pink bedroom in his house and I could sleep there when I wanted."

I'd four magazines read.

"Did you face him?"

"No," she admitted, "but it was only because he was sleeping with his mouth open and I couldn't get his head manoeuvred into position. He walked the last bit home so his mother couldn't smell drink off his breath."

She was simpering. I felt vaguely sick.

"How do I love you, Paddy, let me count the ways. Better still, let me show you."

And I suppose she had.

"He's a real screw," she said. "I can just imagine his eyes raping me."

I was not prepared to tell her that I often imagined them doing the same to me. I said, "Well, the careers officer at school says he should be a sales rep when he grows up. He sounds like a randy bugger to me, Sonia."

"Goody gumdrops," said Sonia. "Marian, will you tell Paddy that I fancy him, and I'll meet him behind the hockey pavilion some lunch-time next week (grovel, grovel)?"

"Never chase a man, Sonia," I said crossly, "They can smell desperation. It's one of Life's Golden Rules."

"I'm not chasing him," said my incorrigible friend. "You're doing it for me."

8

I never felt very jealous of Sonia (though sometimes it was difficult) because, when we were fourteen, her big brother Neil was knocked down and killed walking home from a rugby disco. The scrum half who killed him was drink-driving and became anorexic afterwards. Neil's head was so badly smashed, a white veil covered his face in the coffin. For weeks afterwards, when *Abide With Me* was sung in school assembly, his girlfriend would dissolve into hysterical tears and have to be helped out. It couldn't have helped that he'd two-timed her that fateful night with a fourth former.

Sonia was much too tough to cry in public but, after they switched off the life-support machine, she didn't come back to school for a long time even though Lynette and Darren Anderson, the "Wee Ones" were back in school the day after the funeral. When she returned, she announced that she'd decided not to believe in God so she wouldn't be coming to First Communion classes with me anymore. I remember flicking desperately though my Bible, trying to find a text that would comfort her and begging God fervently on my knees at night to perform some miracle so that she'd believe in Him again.

She'd been such an inspiration to us weaker disciples. A real "Fight the Good Fight" Christian. Once in biology, when we were doing evolution and the homework question was, "What would be the evolutionary significance if gentlemen preferred blondes?" Paddy Butler asked her if she was a "Born Again" in a sniggering voice. And bold as brass she'd said, "Yes I am, Paddy. What are you going to do about it?"

She wasn't even struck down for the blasphemy of choosing not to believe in God. She got eight As in her O levels. Very tedious.

For an unhealthy period after his death, I fantasised that I was Neil's tragic girlfriend who sat day and night beside his hospital bed until he died.

Months before his death I'd spotted him reading a novel on the rugby bus while his team mates mooned out of the windows. I promptly stopped fretting that none of the boys in my class fancied me and fell in puppy love with him.

First love was an awful pain. My crush was so severe I couldn't even share it with Sonia who would have laughed. Which was a pity because the essential elements in any crush, love and pain, are so much more bearable when shared. The bother I went to acquiring his timetable – Sonia could have saved me all that and pinched one from his bedroom. The timetable enabled me to accidentally on purpose be walking past certain classroom doors when he was exiting. I had this wonderful fantasy that one day we would collide in the corridor, and I would be concussed, and he would gather me into his arms and take me to sick bay. Secretly I studied the science of rugby from a library book, so I could travel with him to rugby matches (as Guest of a Rugby Boy) and shout intelligent things at him from the touchline.

One day he actually did sit beside me on the bus home from school and I was in such a spasm of nervous panic, I behaved as if I couldn't see him. I couldn't even trust myself to say "Hello, Neil" without dribbling all over him. He'd been going strong with Stephanie Bruce whose father owned a garage. They shared a radiator at lunch-time outside the history rooms. I remember breathing shallowly and desperately on the bus (my glasses steamed up), and telling myself that he didn't even realise that a frog like me existed. Then he smiled and said, "Hello, Marian, you little mouse." And of course, I melted. Because nothing in the world resembles a little mouse less than me. "Marian, you big saggy sofa," would have been more appropriate.

"Hello, Neil," I squeaked, wringing the moisture from my palms. But I couldn't think of another thing to say to him. To this day, I still wake at night and wonder what intelligent and unforgettable comment I might have made.

He was knocked down and killed less than a week later.

Sonia became so badly spoilt that she was allowed to wear make-up and go out with boys before she was sixteen. The boys would phone Mrs Anderson and ask her permission, but it was only a formality because Mrs Anderson was so devastated by Neil's death that she took to her bed and let Sonia run wild. Neglect is not good loving. She was allowed to take Nicholas Stewart, son of a self-made millionaire, to the caravan in Portrush for the weekend. They'd only been going out together for three weeks. People used to think Nicholas was gay because he went out shooting at the weekends instead of playing rugby.

"He's the most mature and interesting person in our class," Sonia defended herself. "As well as the richest. And he'd be a very good rugby player if he wasn't a better shot."

Better the devil you know, I say. Sonia worried afterwards that, though she'd worn pyjamas and Nicholas had worn pyjamas, they had slept together in the double bed and, even though she was doing O level biology and should know better, it might still be possible to get pregnant through clothes.

I was pure scandalised when she confided in me and told her in no uncertain terms that, though everyone was really sorry that Neil died, her reputation would be on the rocks if she wasn't careful. Boys were only after One Thing.

Sonia laughed at the time and said she was more worried about the "Anderson family eyebrows" than her reputation. Even though she'd tried the "hairspray on the toothbrush" trick, it hadn't worked. They still had a bushy life of their own. Young and dashing Mr Sterling sent us out of biology for talking. He said Sonia was disturbing the boys. One other time he said, "Stop snogging Paddy Butler, Sonia," to her outside the biology labs and Paddy was only touching her arm. Sonia thought Mr Sterling was after her. He was young and it wouldn't have been the first time a teacher fell in love with his student.

Even if it was against school rules.

chapter two

My mother suffered from galloping PMT. She sat at the kitchen table eating bowl after bowl of cornflakes, hoping it would fill the gap. Automatically she nagged at me.

"Don't you dare drink coffee in the lounge, Marian, you'll spill it everywhere."

It was a game we played. She treated me like a retarded twelve-year-old. I stuck my nose in the air and made a point of ignoring her. The Silent Treatment, I called it.

"Sulking again?" she would sneer from behind the box of cereal.

No answer.

"Snobby bag," she'd say next. "You really do try to cut yourself off from the family, Marian. I think you prefer other people to your own family."

Still no answer. I was winning. She only won when she made me cry.

"You're cold and unaffectionate," she'd scream, flinging the cornflakes packet at my head. "I know people who studied to be doctors at a kitchen table with ten youngsters running round them."

This was an amazing fact only she knew. I wish I'd had the imagination to record her for posterity. A character study in respectability. Husband with a nice job, herself with a nice house in a nice private estate, squeaky clean children, squeaky clean life. Nothing to worry about. No wonder she was such a monster, with nothing to do and all day to do it in. No clouds blowing on her horizon. She knew life was selling her short, but she didn't know what was being left out. If Mrs Anderson had been in the same boat she would have been on her second gin and a pack of fags.

She was a pitiful creature, my mother, gobbling secretly at cornflakes, looking at her watch, wondering how much longer it was going to last. She wasn't really a bad person. She'd just got into the habit of being twisted and cross about everything. Why bother saying something nice, when it was as easy to say something nasty? Why say that Sonia was smart, athletic and talented when she could say, justifiably, that she was overbearing, domineering and immature instead.

I couldn't argue with her because we weren't equals. I tried it once and she threw a complete wobbly (and the cereal plate instead of the box of cornflakes), and screamed, "I'm your mother and I do the shouting."

So I used the Silent Treatment and she'd taunt, "You're so nice, Marian, you even fart rose petals." Instead of laughing I would run away and cry and feel another boil growing at the end of my nose.

Once, having listened to *Land of Hope and Glory* on the wireless and feeling "something, I don't know what it is," she told me she thought we would be better friends when I became more mature and more like her. I promised myself I'd jump off a high building if that ever happened.

Sonia and I waitressed at *The Rainbow's End* at weekends. The money was crap but no one else would take us because of the hockey matches on Saturday mornings. My Christian Conscience nagged a bit at the start. It said I shouldn't have been waitressing on a Sunday. Sunday was a day of rest. "Sew on a Sunday, rip it out with your nose on a Monday."

I consulted my Bible for divine permission, opening it at random and reading an unfortunate piece in the Old Testament about a woman being stoned at a Hebrew well for drawing water on the Sabbath.

I asked the advice of the speaker at the presbytery youth weekend in Newcastle but he said he hadn't a clue about the situation.

I became desperate. The only alternative occupation at sixteen was to help out in a burger van at a couple of band parades. And sweat curry chips and onion rings into my school uniform all week afterwards. This was when my mother threw the cereal plate. I told her I'd requested an interview with Rev. Simms to ask him to make the decision for me. She knew as well as I did that Rev. Simms was a hardline stick-in-the-mud who wouldn't eat an egg a hen had laid on a Sunday. And she also knew that as a communicant member it was religious etiquette for me to obey him.

So she threw the cereal bowl and said she wasn't going to have any daughter of hers gallivanting round the country associating with riff-raff at band parades. And, if I didn't waitress, I wouldn't have any money because she wasn't going to fork out for "girl things" for me. A Christian Conscience was a luxury I couldn't afford at sixteen, she said.

It was Sonia who thought of a compromise, even if compromise was the work of the devil. She suggested I give my Sunday waitressing blood-money to the church. My Christian Conscience didn't protest. My mother even compromised to a degree. She drove me to work in the afternoon provided I stayed overnight with Sonia afterwards.

It gave her an opportunity to play the guilt trip record in the car every week. The one about never having educated children because they turned out lazy and didn't clean bathrooms, or wash dishes, and would only do the ironing when the gun was at their heads.

Piqued by her lack of respect for me, self-righteous indignation and rebellion would flutter in my breast. I'd never given her a moment's worry in my life. I'd never broken a plate washing up, or left a ring round the bath. She was nothing but a nagging, dissatisfied, discontented old hag. And I'd arrive at *The Rainbow's End* with another boil at the end of my nose.

She only ever drove me home from work once, and I've regretted screaming, "Come and get me this minute," down the phone at her ever since.

She didn't appear at the appointed hour and she still wasn't there half an hour later.

Finally, she arrived. I got into the car. She drove down the road out of sight of the restaurant and beat me round the head in a frenzied passion.

"What's the matter with you? I've been running after you all week."

I wept weakly in the corner of the passenger seat and thought that by God (if it wasn't blasphemous), that was the last piece of smuggled pavlova she would ever get.

Sonia and I flipped a coin when we started work. Heads I cleaned the toilets, tails she did. Every week. We both hated cleaning. It was one of the few things we had in common.

"Cleanliness is next to Godliness, Marian," she said when it was tails. "You should be volunteering to do bog duty."

She was always cheerful on a Saturday because Big Shirley usually let her off early to go to *Kate's* (the pub for under-age alcoholics). And maybe Paddy Butler would be there and they could repeat the cannibalistic court of Thursday night, and she might get another lovebite on her bottom.

"A tattoo would be less painful," I told her.

She looked at me pityingly. "And less fun," she said.

I never asked to go home early on Saturday night. I valued my pound an hour too much. Anyway, I wasn't allowed to go to *Kate's* – riff-raff hung out there too, lurking behind pillars taking advantage of nice girls (like me?), my mother said.

I had a serious problem at seventeen. Not only did I obey my mother, I even listened to her.

It was the football club's Christmas dinner dance that night and Jonathan Lamb started work at 5 pm. Wee Lamb was a nobody who'd been in the year above us at school (this meant he didn't play rugby). He was studying accountancy at Queen's but came home every weekend with his washing. It was rumoured that he was very domesticated and hung out his mother's washing. He brought me a cup of coffee in the laundry room and sympathised with the cuts on my knees from falling over my feet at hockey.

"Hi," Sonia whispered when she finished cleaning and I was making her coffee. "Hi, Marian, I think Wee Lamb fancies you. Didn't I hear him asking you if you were going to the school Christmas dance, because he was going, and didn't I see him feeling your leg in the laundry room?"

Sniggering Sonia. One cup of coffee and, provided he wasn't a rugby boy, there were wedding bells in the air. If he was a rugby boy she wasted no time telling you to keep off her patch.

"It's true," she declared prophetically. "He wants to go with you but he's too shy to ask you properly."

"Do you think," I asked, haughty with embarrassment, "that I'd go out with a boy who was shorter than me?"

"Beggars can't be choosers," she sniggered. "I can count the number of boys you've faced on the fingers of one hand, Marian."

The finger of one hand would have been more

accurate and that was only when Jimmy Fingers stuck his tongue down my throat for a dare in fourth year.

I took a good look at Wee Lamb again. Our fingers touched when we were setting the tables in the function room and I got a flash. Impulsively I decided that he did not have the shortest legs in the . . . whole world. He was a small boy, but beautifully formed and being a mummy's boy would come in handy when it came to winning my mother round. He was probably as shy and desperate with members of the opposite sex as I was so he wouldn't be able to tell that I didn't know how to kiss, or flirt, or do "girl things."

He asked Sonia about her hockey match. Sonia said the opposition were wimpy. Quietly he said, "Just like me." He wasn't kidding or trying to seek attention or anything. Then, later, as it was a full moon, Sonia was on about turning into a werewolf. He said, "I just turn green, boring as usual."

My mother went on like that on her PMT days. It usually ended with a tirade about her having feelings too. Jonathan and she would get along fine. I'd go a long way to find another boy with such nice manners and clean fingernails.

So, when he smiled and asked me if I'd like another cup of coffee, I smiled straight back at him and said, "Yes, please, Jonathan." It was a start, anyway.

One hundred and twenty people were eating at the football club's dinner dance, and, guess what, they burned the dinners. All that roast beef and turkey and thousands, or was it millions, starving in Africa. Instead of eating at half eight, the footballers ate at ten. Not good for business, you would have thought, but they couldn't get the drink down their throats fast enough so they didn't notice the time passing. Things were so tight that Big Shirley plucked Sonia from the dining-room and went over the ins and outs of the bar with her. Shake, tremble, quiver.

"Right Sonia, it's all yours," she said, and I was left to the mercy of the Bimbo Sisters who never washed a dish. Stupid bleeps. I never felt more like quitting.

Sonia was in a mood too. Big Shirley had cancelled her early night and she was fretting that Paddy Butler would be autographing someone else's buttock.

"Seldom seen, often admired," I whispered during the raffle, a temporary lull, but she was beyond comfort.

"Five full bottles of vodka drunk already," she scowled, "and the disco unit hasn't arrived yet."

"Do you want to work next Saturday night?" Big Shirley joked when we were leaving, exhausted. My nose had swollen halfway across my face with tiredness. "It's a youth presbytery party. Non-alcoholic indulgence to the excess."

Sonia drove us home slowly through lashing rain and high winds. She talked steadily so neither of us could mention Neil. "Out of sight, out of mind," my foot. Neil was dead three years at that stage. I think people never really get over a death. They just learn to live with it.

"It doesn't look like it's going to be a white Christmas this year again," I said, but she was thinking about Paddy Butler.

"It's so bloody annoying, Marian," she said. "Yesterday I was sitting opposite him in the sixth form study room and we were alone together, and he ignored me. Great. Fine. Super. Why could he not have asked to borrow my ruler or something and brought the chat round to the rugby disco, or maybe the school dance? Do you think he doesn't like me any more?"

"Of course he still likes you," I said lamely. Paddy Butler liked everything in a skirt. A Romeo and a B category man, it was a very easy to like him back again. I didn't think it was the time or place to confess that he'd wanted to take me outside the night of the LoveBite on the Bum. I never intended to cross swords with Sonia over the head of a rugby boy. It was a Golden Rule that friends always came first. That was probably why I never had a boyfriend.

"Well at least I didn't lower myself to talk to him," said Sonia. "I'm not going to make the same mistake with Paddy as I did with Nicholas Stewart."

That episode in the caravan, it was best forgotten. I knew the whole story. Nicholas had been more nervous than her. She slept in flannelette pyjamas and knickers and a T-shirt, Nicholas wore pyjamas and a sweatshirt. After an experimental feel of her bust, he rolled over and went to sleep.

Why had we worried about her being pregnant? Because Nicholas admitted to getting sexually aroused by her fingers on the back of his neck?

"Imagine having to face the rest of your life with the stigma of being an unmarried mother," Sonia said at the time. "And not even the memory of a bit of mindless passion to comfort yourself."

Nicholas claimed afterwards that he still respected Sonia as a lady. But he never asked her out again. She made a bit of a fool of herself by chasing after him for the weeks up till her period arrived.

I remember telling her, "I can't imagine that you could have been impregnated and be asleep and not feel a thing, Sonia. If it is the case, medical science will undoubtedly take you under their wing when your mother throws you out of the house."

Then, to lighten the heavy chat, I'd suggested we stick pillows up under our jumpers to see what we'd look like pregnant.

Once Sonia's period arrived we were rational enough to realise that only a contortionist could have deflowered her in such circumstances.

After the initial shock, I was extremely understanding about the caravan affair and vowed I'd never tell a soul. A child of my mother's, I had a healthy respect for gossip-mongers, tittle-tattle, and keeping up appearances. And for "The Reputation."

According to my mother, the reputation was like a delicate flower needing constant attention. Turn your back on it once, and you lost it forever. A pity one's Christian Conscience was more of a thistle.

When we arrived at the farm Sonia said, "Marian, I think a true friend would tell Paddy Butler that her best friend fancied him."

I said, "According to Jonathan Lamb, the male's sex-drive is ten times that of the female. So I shouldn't try any hanky-panky with Paddy Butler."

Mrs Anderson had left Sonia a note sellotaped to the back door. "I steeped the laces of your baseball boots and they came up lovely and white. Did you bring a doggy-bag?"

Mrs Anderson was the most charismatic and terrifying woman I'd ever met. Like a bright colour or a loud bang vibrating in the memory. She was brittle, insincere and beautiful, a huge plastic sunflower planted in a field of dandelions and dried grass. She treated Sonia and Lynette with a charming and detached friendliness. They were always polite to each other but, in a line-up of teenage girls, it's doubtful if she would have recognised either of them. Neil was a different matter. She became professionally manic after he died. I wasn't particularly sensitive but I could feel her depression hanging round her like a shroud, and it frightened me.

When we came into the kitchen, Lynette was sitting beside the Aga in a sea of holly, plaiting it deftly into wreaths, which she sold at the market on Thursday, for people to put on graves at Christmas. She was quite pretty at fifteen but she was at the bright shiny nose stage and she cried a lot. Sonia said she was "a nasty wee squirt" and treated her like an imbecile. But I'd have said, even then, that she had more brains than the rest of us put together.

She said, "Do you know what I saw Darren playing with in the bath tonight? At least it means he's too big to play with Action Man now."

Sonia ignored her and I tried to hide my shock at a family who didn't bolt the bathroom door. Everything was bolted in our house. I have a brother, Stephen, and he scuttled from a locked bedroom to a locked bathroom and back again for maybe ten years when he was growing up. "I suppose you were in the bathroom looking at yourself in the mirror again," Sonia said nastily.

They all thought Lynette fancied some boy because she never stopped looking at herself in the mirror.

"Aren't you just lucky I fancy a boy?" said Lynette. "If I fancied a girl you'd really have something to worry about." I heard her singing, "Sisters, there were never such devoted sisters," as she ran up the stairs.

"I caught that wee skitter reversing the Vauxhall Nova round the house yesterday," said Sonia. "I gave her a real hard wallop with my hockey stick, her fingers are black and blue."

I never slept very well at Anderson's house because I was always afraid that Mrs Anderson would knife me in the middle of the night. My mother told me not to be so stupid when I told her. And of course I couldn't tell Sonia in case she'd be offended. So I left shoes and things scattered about the floor to trip her up if she came for me.

In my nervous half sleep that night I dreamt about Paddy Butler, Catholic Butler. His lists of conquests read like a war memorial. He should have had a public health warning slapped on him, you know, but even I could understand Sonia's fascination for him. Nice middle-class girls like us were often attracted to charming riff-raff like

24

Butler. We saw ourselves as reforming angels, "I was the girl who changed him from being a drunken philanderer into a decent boyfriend." Which was a bit silly, on reflection. For if you fancied him when he was a drunken philanderer, could you really still fancy him decent?

Being Catholic, and forbidden fruit in our community, Butler was in danger of getting his head kicked in for facing Sonia. Had Neil Anderson still been alive it would have been his duty to warn Butler off. "Touch my sister and you die."

I dreamt Paddy was lying on the road with boys in black balaclavas kicking him. One of the boys had a white veil over his face and, when he lifted it, it was Neil. I saw his face as clearly as if he was standing in front of me, smiling his big adorable smile.

I woke in a cold sweat, but I don't think Sonia heard me. I didn't want it to be like that. I wished I could forget. But I couldn't.

chapter three

The school dance was the highlight of our school year. The boys wore fancy dress and the girls were dolled up to the nines. Preparations, romantic and cosmetic, often started weeks in advance. So many boys, so little time.

I was working on Jonathan Lamb.

"Are you going to the school dance, Jonathan?"

"Yes, Marian, I am, are you?"

"Yes, Jonathan, I am."

Pregnant pause and the both of us smiling and blushing and wondering what to do next.

My dress was a black and grey peep-hole creation with a black bow on the bum (guess what that was to hide!). I'd been trying to diet – eating chewing gum when I felt hungry, and walking on my bum up and down the hall at home to shift the beef.

"My front view's OK," I explained to Sonia, who was fed up listening to me. "But my backside really is still far too big, even after all the bum-walking exercises."

The charming Sonia said the problem was not my weight but my posture. She said I had an hour-glass figure but, because I was flat-footed, I tended to waddle along as if I'd just wet myself. "Like a ewe with a water bag, Marian," she said once but I didn't think that was funny.

I just couldn't bear the picky women at *The Rainbow's End* who didn't make an honest attempt to clear their plates. It was one of Life's Golden Rules: "A real lady should have a healthy appetite, stemming from a healthy life, yet she should never stuff herself, or say 'I'm stuffed'."

With such an attitude it was little wonder I was on the plump side of pleasant.

Sonia wore a red monstrosity she got in Liverpool on hockey tour. All lace with enormous shoulder pads. I didn't appreciate it much. The sight of it brought back ugly memories. The whole hockey tour had been a nightmare for me. I even scored an own goal in one match, stupid bleep. To make matters worse, I'd been yapping at everyone else before it happened.

Sonia got really irritated with me complaining that the price of the peep-hole dress had me bankrupt. On the last night, when everyone else was pigging out on a slap-up Chinese, I could only afford a cup of coffee. I said it was through choice, not necessity, when she offered me a loan.

"You have to suffer to be beautiful," I said, saliva dripping off my chin as I watched her scoff down sweet-and-sour pork.

"Buy a bigger dress and keep eating," she advised.

She'd asked Paddy Butler to the dance. Nothing subtle there.

"Listen, Paddy," she said, "I'm only going to say this once, will you come to the school dance with me?"

"No."

Sonia wasn't easily defeated. She faced life courageously, and with imagination. The day of the dance, when I was buying a girdle to compress my bottom, she convinced herself that he'd just taken stage fright.

She went to *Curl Up and Dye* and got her hair blown dry (£3.50). She bought a pair of black lace gloves (£2.99) and a new bra (£1.99).

And, while I wrestled with the girdle, she put on fake tan and painted her toenails. "That chipped and cheap-looking nail varnish must be a phase you're going through," I said.

Astringent, moisturiser, spot concealer, foundation, translucent powder. Her eyes were green pearl on the lids, pink pearl on the brows, with cream brushed over it, green eyeliner along the lower lashes, browny-black mascara, pale pink blusher and pale pink lipstick.

The Anderson family eyebrows were plucked into a thin line. Lynette watched us through a crack in the door. She'd tried to enter but Sonia had grabbed a pair of scissors and threatened to cut her breasts off.

"That wee snig needs a thump," she said when I protested that, really, Lynette would be doing no harm watching. It's very boring being fifteen and waiting to grow up. When we were ready Sonia advised me to leave my halo at home. She sneaked a Lucozade bottle full of vodka and coke past Mr Sterling at the door. He could hardly have strip searched a sixth form girl even if he was doing a thorough job on the boys.

Paddy was dressed as the Emperor Nero. He wore a white pillowcase round his reproductive organs. The pillowcase barely covered his behind and he was the hairiest person any of us had ever seen. On Sonia's instructions I took a photograph of him with her pretending to stick her tongue in his ear.

But he was firmly attached to Stephanie Bruce, Neil's old girlfriend, now our esteemed head girl.

"Is Stephanie in fancy dress?" Sonia whispered to me, throwing her a dirty look. "That pink wool dress does nothing for her. Her buttocks are bigger than yours, Marian."

You could tell she was wondering if Stephanie's buttock was also brand-marked.

We watched Jimmy Fingers ask her to dance and Paddy say, "Leave my girlfriend alone, Fingers." Maybe it was a joke.

"Look at the pair of them," Sonia said (madly jealous). "They're just a couple that nobody wants."

I've said it before, Sonia was no oil painting, but at least she had a couple of desirable features. Nobody knew what phylum Stephanie belonged to. I think she was quite pretty when she was Neil Anderson's girlfriend but now she looked like an overweight man. Sonia still only had to mention Neil's name for Stephanie to burst into tears. People think that because you're fifteen when your boyfriend dies it shouldn't hurt as much. And even less so because he two-timed her. She carried the whole thing closed up inside her and grew fat and ugly on it.

I boogied a bit at the start with Jimmy Fingers because I didn't have any choice and he was dancing near Jonathan Lamb (who had come as a waiter with the lingering smell of fried chicken hanging to him).

Jimmy was dressed as a dirty old man.

"Do you have anything beneath that lab coat, Fingers?" I asked him nervously.

"No," said Fingers, unmoved.

"Well, keep it closed, then," I snapped.

"We have a purely platonic relationship, Marian," he told me condescendingly. "I'm very selective in my flashing."

Well, call me old-fashioned but, if he didn't fancy me, why couldn't I get rid of him? Every time I turned round he was wanting to dance with me. His lips felt like cold bacon under the mistletoe. At least he didn't try to choke me with his tongue like in fourth year.

Sonia was having a "brilliant time", to quote Jimmy. I almost tripped over her lying in the middle of the dance floor watching the band who were pretty groovy even if all their songs were copies (they played nothing original).

During one song Jonathan tapped me on the shoulder and grinned into my face. It may have been his little way of saying he fancied me. I smiled brightly and said, "Hello, Jonathan," which was my little way of saying I fancied him.

Sonia dragged me to the toilets while we stood and smiled and blushed at each other.

"Stephanie Bruce, or no Stephanie Bruce, I have a very strong feeling Paddy Butler still wants me," said Sonia. "God, I feel like a virgin nymphomaniac or maybe I'm on heat, I'm so frustrated. All I can think about are Paddy's hands touching me and him eating the mouth clean off me."

She turned a flamboyant cartwheel and did a handstand up against the wall of a locked cubicle so her red lace monstrosity dress fell down over her ears. I smoothed the peep-hole creation dress down over my hips and squirmed a bit. Pagan confessions embarrassed me. I couldn't even kiss.

It was perhaps unfortunate that the locked cubicle contained The Gorgon Sisters, three of the deadliest bitches at our school. Gorgon wasn't their real surname, of course, and they weren't even sisters, but Sonia said they were just like the three dolls in Greek mythology who shared a tooth and eye between them.

Mandy Gorgon faced Neil Anderson the night he was knocked down.

"Someone should tell her," Sonia said at the time, "that she's stupid-looking with all that foundation on her face."

In junior school, when bullying was a physical thing, I had been terrorised by them. Mandy Gorgon stole my lunch box once and ate all my sandwiches and left a note saying how much she enjoyed them; Lorraine Gorgon put my fluffy pencil-case under a dripping tap in the chemistry labs; Donna Gorgon pulled my mother-of-pearl bangle off my wrist and threw it down the toilet (and I had to go in after it).

What those three ladies needed at fourteen was their asses kicked up their throats and manners beat into them. But I'd been too nicely brought up to even consider asking Sonia to do it for me. Sonia was an artist with her hockey stick, both on and off the pitch. I like to think that one word from me and Gorgon grey matter would have sprayed the junior toilets. Instead I swept the nastiness under the carpet and hid when I saw them coming. Of course they didn't go away. When we reached sixth form they became too mature to break rulers and hide calculators, and graduated to mental torture. My ears burned when I walked past them in the school corridor. Even when they didn't say anything.

So when they emerged from the locked cubicle, my knees started to knock unattractively. They were laughing maniacally, but Sonia got her say in first. You could always depend on Sonia to sink as low as was necessary in a Gorgon skirmish. Dignity was a waste of time in battle.

"The Gorgons." She clapped her hands. "Wonderful costumes, darlings. You're the witches in *Macbeth*, aren't you?" She took my arm to frogmarch me out of the toilets.

"That trio," she said loudly. "I'd be careful, Marian. I think they're lesbians the way they're always in the toilet together."

Jonathan Lamb was waiting for me at the door of the disco. Spontaneously he asked me to dance. It was about a quarter past eleven. Jim Diamond was singing *I Should Have Known Better*.

Jonathan said, "Awh well, we might as well" and put his arms round me. Be still, my beating heart. He wasn't that short after all. We danced quite awkwardly for a few minutes and Jonathan said, "We're going to regret this tomorrow, but it is Christmas." He then gently tried to wangle a kiss but, as I still couldn't kiss and was too shy to try, we ended up dancing with our noses touching. Then we kissed and kissed and kissed.

After that hurdle? It was fabulous fun and really easy after all. Well, talk about leeches, it must have been really amusing to watch. We even danced ear to ear at a point. We kept our arms round each other the rest of the night, even when the fast dances started later. The Pointer Sisters song *I'm so Excited* was on and when the bit "squeeze you, wrap my arms around you" came on that's exactly what Jonathan did. The nicest kiss, though, was when he ran his hands up and down my back while we kissed. It was a class feeling. He kissed my neck while we were dancing but I was terrified of getting a lovebite – talk about squirming!

I was desperately in love with Jonathan that night, and not a bit desperate.

And I managed to miss Sonia making a prize exhibition of herself.

She and Paddy were dirty-dancing, real "Come and get me" stuff as the clock struck twelve. She was shaking with excitement because every move he made in her direction made her stomach contract with nerves.

In a moment of mad and reckless passion she said, "Come out to the car for a bonk, Paddy."

Paddy, who was out of his tree, said, "Not tonight, dear, I've got a headache." Then he dashed back to Stephanie Bruce and snogged her. After he'd finished with Stephanie, he wiped his mouth and kissed a Gorgon.

One thing about Sonia, she never learned to cope with rejection. She bounded across the dance floor to where Paddy was revving up to kiss another Gorgon, and punched him on the mouth. Sonia was always her own worst enemy. She threw herself on Jimmy Fingers who was hovering on the edge of the action, clutching a bunch of mistletoe, hoping someone would include him in the kissing orgy and said, "I'm a poser, Fingers, let's dance in the middle of the floor, so everyone can see that I don't care who Paddy Butler faces."

That duty done she disappeared down to the cloakroom and I didn't see her till we were ready for home.

"What's wrong, Sonia?" I said when Jonathan and I unstuck ourselves at the end of the night. "Are you going to be sick?" There were two big tears in her eyes. Not a good sign. "If you're going to be sick," I said, "you'll have to go home with Jimmy Fingers."

We were bad to Fingers at school. Nobody cared if they were sick in the back seat of his car. After the last rugby disco, a rugby boy was so sick out of the window that my mother, driving behind, had to use her windscreen wipers. Jimmy washed the car out afterwards and didn't complain. Ha, Ha, up his with parsley sauce.

Adolescent friendship is a symbiotic thing. Sonia and I were like two parasites feeding off each other. The only time I ever really liked her was when I was in love with her brother Neil. And she has often said that I bored the tits off her at seventeen.

"I don't know why you're so worked up," I said huffily. "Paddy only kissed Stephanie. You can never trust a boy who carries condoms in his school blazer."

She had downed the whole bottle of vodka and coke in one mouthful in the cloakroom.

"Amazing fact, Marian – I can't see my reflection when I'm drunk," said Sonia. "Then I think I must have passed out, because the next thing I remember is waking up on the ground and Mr Sterling's shoes beside my face."

"What was he doing in the girls' toilets?" I demanded.

"He was checking for smokers, I suppose," said Sonia. "He carried me outside to puke my guts out, and do you know what he said? He said, 'If you vomit on my shoes, Sonia, I'll shit a brick.' If he ever loved me, I bet he promptly stopped."

"Why can't you cry into your hanky like everyone else?" I asked crossly.

"It's one of the Golden Rules, or have you forgotten, Marian? Smile Though Your Heart is Breaking."

"Jonathan kisses with his eyes closed and he's just the same height as me with my pop-ons on," I said. "But I think I'll wear flat shoes in future when we're out together."

She wasn't listening to me. What did Sonia care if Jonathan Lamb had proposed marriage to me? He wasn't a rugby boy, and he wasn't Paddy Butler.

"I don't want to ever see Paddy Butler again," Sonia screamed passionately. "I want you to tell him that I don't want him to speak to me, or smile at me, or look at me ever again, Marian."

"Quite right too," I lectured. "Reverend Simms says that having communion and fellowship with Catholics is wrong, in fact it's a sin. The Virgin Mary is not important. And it could have been worse, Sonia, he could have faced a Gorgon."

One thing you had to admire about the Gorgons was their mobilisation of resources. A Gorgon didn't cry in her handkerchief. They were Mistresses of Making The Best Of A Bad Evening. Lorraine and Donna shared Jimmy Fingers between them at the end of the night. Nobody dared suggest they were desperate and he was Any Port In a Storm. A black eye would have been such a mess over Christmas.

"But I'm still crazy about him," screamed the irrational Sonia, who was slumped on the toilet seat, her red dress round her ankles. "It's so difficult to stop all of a sudden."

Her new bra was red with dye from the dress. She said she'd dreamed she was facing him the whole three hours she was asleep and woke almost too exhausted to be sick again into the bathroom sink. She pushed the vomit through the plug hole with a toothbrush.

She looked crap the whole way through the school

carol service. Talk about laying it on. Pathetic, really. No one was treating her differently, but maybe she just felt different inside. It made me uncomfortable to watch Sonia Star behaving like a normal girl. Sonia was the original "I'll bust you" tomboy who wore man-catching clothes. The one who teased me about boys, and teased the boys too.

It was the calm before the storm.

After the carol service, when we were packing up for Christmas and Jimmy Fingers was dancing to *Nellie the Elephant* in the middle of the sixth form centre, she grabbed a milk bottle.

"You're nothing but a dirty low dog, Paddy Butler!" she screamed. "Go and jump off a high cliff into a deep part of the ocean." And she broke the milk bottle over his head.

So, while Jonathan held my hand inside his coat pocket and carried my schoolbag up the street for me, Sonia was wrapping Paddy's head in her woolly tights and taking him to Casualty across the playing-fields. It had been trying to snow and she said afterwards that she pushed him down and fell on top of him on the sleety grass and kissed him.

Jonathan and I talked about everything (and I mean everything) in *The Cobbled Courtyard* coffee shop. He let me pay, he took a wee bit of sugar with black coffee. My mother said she saw us and paraded up and down in front of the coffee shop watching that he didn't play footsie with me (he didn't). We talked until half past four when he walked me home, and I made him more coffee and we shut the door into the kitchen to keep my mother and Stephen out. Eventually we started kissing. He managed to arouse me in thirty seconds just by rubbing noses. I got aroused afterwards just thinking about it.

We were both much more relaxed after the first kiss. He said he was shy making the first move but that I was a fantastic kisser and his hands started to wander, and, nervously, I let them above my jumper.

He said he hadn't slept a wink all night thinking about me. He looked at me in that heart-rending way with his eyebrow raised that embarrassed me so much and made me think that maybe there was more to life after all than being Guest of a Rugby Boy.

chapter four

There's nothing more depressing than an anticlimax Christmas. I thought it was going to be great for me that year because I had a boyfriend. It was my stupid bloody family spoiled it. How can you expect young girls to believe in marrying for love when they hear nothing but wives constantly nagging about their husbands' inadequacies. Daddy had his office dinner on Christmas Eve and my mother caused a terrible scene because he didn't take her. He showed a most violent temper and tipped the tea table and beat her round the head and hurt her.

I scattered to choir practice with cold tears stinging my face and my hood up so no one could see. That's what was wrong with our house. No one brought their problems into the open. We bitched behind backs, petty squabbles, yap, yap, yap. Then there was a periodic blow-out when someone got battered, usually me or my mother.

Sonia was also suffering Christmas Blues.

"Do you have a rope, Marian?"

"What do you want a rope for?" A reasonable enough question on Christmas Eve on the last run through of *The Holly and the Ivy*.

"I want to hang myself," said Sonia. "Paddy Butler hasn't phoned me."

Oh, God, I thought (if it wasn't blasphemous), here we go again. Will I just tell her that she's making a gullible prat of herself running after him, and everybody's laughing at her because they know he's only with her for the good bit he gets at the end of the night, and he's two-timing her with Mandy Gorgon, I saw them with my own eyes at the back of the pictures. And she'll never speak to me again, and I'll never have to listen to another Paddy Butler story again and I'll never bask in her reflected glory again.

I said nothing. Without Sonia's light on my face I would have been in shadow all my life.

"He must be a brilliant actor," Sonia persisted, somewhat desperately. "I thought he was fond of me. He was so attentive the day of the carol service making sure I didn't get my feet wet in the sleet walking home."

Mrs Mulholland stopped playing the organ and glared at me. She had sonic eardrums, Mrs Mulholland.

"Miss Marian," she said, "perhaps we'll have your solo of *Little Donkey* now."

I turned on her. Flushing, I said, "Certainly, Mrs Mulholland, but I rather think the high bits in *The Holly and the Ivy* need more work. What a pity the other worthy disciples of the congregation aren't as faithful as me attending choir practice."

I was like a rat in a drain if you cornered me. My Christian Conscience should have done something about it. "We all appreciate your service, Miss Marian," said Mrs Mulholland obsequiously, "especially God."

I hardly slept a wink all night worrying. I could hear my mother crying and saying, "You don't know, I have a massive problem."

On Christmas morning I rose with an inbuilt knowledge that I was going to eat and eat and eat until my stomach burst. This was not the symptom of an eating disorder, of course. Eating disorders were linked to psychological disorders and were typical of over-ambitious teenagers pushing themselves to extremes. You read about them in biology textbooks. It was just that Christmas Day was "Eat-As-Much-As-You-Can-Day" and once anyone overeats, it's natural to develop a "What The Hell" attitude and stuff yourself silly.

Santa hadn't left me any presents so I scoffed the most of Stephen's Selection Box while I ran around like a headless chicken getting dinner ready before I went to church.

My mother sat in her dressing-gown, watching me. Face like collapsed paper, eyes bloodshot, hair sticking to her head. I was shocked by my lack of sympathy for her. Why couldn't she pull herself together and peel the potatoes or something? I chose to forget that Daddy had hit her.

"Are you coming to church?" I asked carefully in the silence.

"No."

"But I'm singing a solo verse in 'Little Donkey'." I wanted to scream. "I wanted you and Daddy and Stephen to come. I wanted us to be like other families on Christmas Day. Even Mrs Anderson goes to church at Christmas and she doesn't believe in God or in Jesus being born in a manger at Bethlehem. She still comes, and last year she wore tinsel in her hair and gave Rev. Simms a bottle of gin on the church steps and said, 'Gin makes you sin, Rev.' and kissed him on the mouth."

"Who am I going to sit beside if you don't come? I want you to come."

I put on my nice sensible burgundy suit, left the button on the waistband open and turned the oven on to cook the tiny turkey before I left.

The Andersons were all wearing Manchester United baseball caps, even Mrs Anderson. "Darren bought us them as Christmas presents," she trilled, air kissing me lavishly.

"I gave £15 to the free-will offering," I told them proudly.

"Guilt money." Sonia screeched with laughter and everybody turned round to look at us. "If you want, Marian, I'll hold that Christian Conscience of yours while you hit it."

"I'm starting to worry that our Sonia was dropped on her head when she was a baby," Lynette whispered to me. "I've got a secret, Marian. Jimmy Fingers was sitting beside me in church and he smiled at me the whole time and fed me the most of his packet of wine gums."

"And I suppose your heart did a million flips?" I said sarcastically.

"Yes, it did," said Lynette seriously. "I'd say I'm totally cracked on him."

You're wasting your time, I thought, he can't kiss.

"He seems very popular with the girls," Lynette persisted, "and he's a real laugh. Will you get me a copy of his school timetable, Marian, so I can follow him round next term and flirt with him?"

"I'll do better than that," I said, for it was the season of goodwill and, even if no one wanted to be my friend, it didn't mean that I couldn't make somebody else happy at Christmas.

"The church party pop group he plays in are performing tomorrow night at the Sunday school Christmas party. I'll get Sonia to take us if you like."

Jonathan was waiting tables at *The Rainbow's End*. I could afford to be generous.

"Oh yuk," said Sonia, when I told her, "but at least it's not someone in the God squad. One of them used to fancy me when we were in third year. He kept hitting me over the head with his file, do you remember?"

"Yes," I said dryly, "and you said you were going to smash his face because he'd tossed your hair."

"If you don't want to go, Lynette and I will go without you," I threatened. Sonia hated to be left out of things.

"I'll never survive till tomorrow, I'm so excited," said Sonia sarcastically.

Christmas dinner was strained. We ate the soup when I got home from church so the meal was not a lengthy or magnificent process. The entire tradition took half an hour. Stephen's nose didn't appear from round his book. I tried and tried to make civilised conversation but everyone was too wrapped up in themselves to answer me. My mother never spoke except to say, "You must be the worst cook in the world, Marian. I can't for the life of me guess what this meat is. Have you the mustard, the cranberry jelly and the HP Sauce on the table to catch us out?"

To compensate she lay on the sofa stuffing her face with cornflakes, crippled with gluttony, while I washed the dishes. Then I ran upstairs and cried as though my heart was breaking.

I was a nice girl, and a good daughter. She had no reason to dislike me.

At least Jonathan wanted me. He'd given me a fine 9-ct gold chain for Christmas, tasteful and gorgeous.

"I saw that chain on special offer in Smyth's of Magherafelt before Christmas," Sonia said when she saw it, "and it cost £32, but I don't think it looks its price."

We were getting ready at her house for the church party. Lynette winked at me. "So, show us what Paddy Butler bought you, Sonia," she sniggered.

She was wearing white boots with her jeans tucked into them and a white ribbon in her hair. She looked like a million dollars but that might have been excitement.

"I cut a chunk out of Sonia's white lacy top to make this ribbon," she whispered to me.

Sonia said, "I wouldn't wear that silly ribbon, Lynette,

if I was you, you don't have nice enough ears, or a nice enough face for that matter."

"And look," I persisted, showing them the padded card he'd given me with his last Rolo stuck to it. "Look what it says, 'To Marian, who is wonderful even if she's too modest to say so.'"

"Pity he didn't leave the silver paper on the sweet," said Sonia spitefully. "It mightn't have melted." She was awful-looking that day, skinny face, puffy eyes, Paddy Butler withdrawal.

She did a handbrake turn in the church car park for badness. "Hi, Lynette," she shouted as we paid our money, "keep your legs crossed, not your fingers."

Lynette homed in on Jimmy Fingers immediately. I'd gone to parties with Sonia since we were in primary school and it was obvious where Lynette got it from. Fingers's hair curls on to his shoulders like Starsky out of *Starsky and Hutch* and he was wearing a pink leather tie. What did Lynette see in him?

For the first game I got a thin boy with shaky hands who kept tying his laces. Sonia was left out, no one picked her. It was a stupid game where the boys walked round the room and the girls stood still. When the boy had two girls, they twisted and then swung the girls round until everyone was so dizzy they fell over. I didn't want the thin boy to be ruptured trying to lift me so I ran out on him at the first opportunity and sat down on Sonia's knee.

"That boy over there, Ian something, he didn't ask me up but he came over and pestered me. That skinny boy you were with, his father's a pervert."

"According to you, everybody's perverted," I laughed.

"Get up," she said suddenly, "you're squashing me."

But she wasn't a bit squashed. Paddy Butler had just walked in the door.

"What's he doing here?" I said. Then I said, "Don't make a fool of yourself, Sonia, he's not worth worrying about." But of course she didn't listen.

Paddy asked me up for *The Waves of Troy*, and Sonia asked the fellow, Ian, she claimed was pestering her.

Paddy Butler the octopus. He kissed me twice on the mouth during *The Waves of Troy* and the second time I kissed him back again. I can hardly remember how it happened. He stuck his hand up my skirt at the back of the church hall and as I struggled to get away (in case Rev. Simms saw and had me excommunicated for indecent exposure, or Sonia saw and never spoke to me again), I fell up against a stack of chairs and Paddy fell on top of me. He pinned me down, looked around, and kissed me. And, possessed by something I didn't have a name for, I kissed him back.

"If you don't get off me," I gasped, for I was as shocked as he was, "I'll run away from you screaming."

Paddy shrugged. "While you're running," he said, "run via Sonia and tell her that I really regret two-timing her and I'd ask her out again only my pride's preventing me."

"Where's Mandy Gorgon?" I asked, watching Sonia. She was the only person I knew who could play a party game with her legs at a 180° angle.

"I finished with her because she wasn't a Christian," he said facetiously.

Within ten minutes she was sitting on his knee at the back of the hall and they were kissing.

Jimmy Fingers finished playing *The Farmer Wants a Wife* and jumped off the stage and disappeared with Lynette. I was half asleep beside a radiator by the time she returned, having already spent twenty minutes queuing for the toilet. I was getting madder by the second. Hardly anybody had come near me and I had almost blended into the wallpaper. It was the couple thing again. There was even incest at church parties.

Come back, Jonathan, all is forgiven. "My boyfriend's buying me dinner tomorrow night at *The Rainbow's End*," I wanted to shout, "which is more than can be said for the rest of you."

"You know Sandra Jackson who's in the Girls' Brigade with me?" said Lynette. "Her eyes nearly popped out of her head when she saw me with Jimmy Fingers. He's a real laugh, Marian. He says he 'set up a try' at the rugby cup match last Wednesday. I wonder what 'set up a try' means. I'm meeting him by the radiators at the history rooms on Monday, when we get back after Christmas."

Jimmy Fingers was on a cloud. Big thrill. He tickled me like mad which made me feel sick.

"Bags I the driver's seat on the way home," I said.

Jonathan arrived for me at 7 on the dot to take me to dinner. He brought a box of *Milk Tray* for my mother. All pleased, she made him a cup of tea and sat watching him while he drank it, beads of perspiration forming on his forehead. He was wearing a leather jacket and driving a Ford Orion so he passed the twenty questions.

We left for *The Rainbow's End* at five to eight, once my mother checked that I wasn't wearing too much make-up. She told me to come home whenever I wanted!

"Aren't I getting so polite?" she whispered as we left. "I know that boy will be good to you." What was putting her in a good mood?

The Rainbow's End was a quaint place with a huge saloon style bar which had almost every drink ever invented. The dining area was behind the bar. There was a huge table stacked with éclairs, lemon meringue pie, trifle, cheesecake, Black Forest gateau, cream, shortcake, yummy!

I felt a sudden flash of happiness. My mother had been nice to me, my boyfriend was buying me dinner. The heavy cloud of Christmas anticlimax lifted long enough for me to smile at Sonia who was waiting our table. Never one to disguise her emotions, she made it quite obvious that she didn't want to be stuck in the rotten *Rainbow's End* waitressing with the Bimbo Sisters. Already one of them had slipped on a pea and broken five turkey dinners she was carrying into the dining area.

"I thought you were going on a diet," she taunted. "You and Jonathan are going to grow into one of those big fattie couples that come in to celebrate every occasion with a slap-up feed."

"You're only jealous," I said, "that I'm fat and happy and you're thin and cross."

Still, I was mindful of Christmas day's binge and the

fact that I weighed almost eleven stones which was too much, even at Christmas. I ordered chicken *chasseur* with boiled potatoes because they were less fattening than chips, and button mushrooms because I was sure I had read in a biology book somewhere that fungi didn't have calories.

Jonathan had sweet and sour pork with patna rice. Delicious. It was just Jonathan's little way that he gave a running commentary about every mouthful.

chapter five

Then one day I stopped fancying Jonathan. We'd been dating for three months and the pictures was the height of my week's excitement. Except I never saw any of it because he didn't want to watch the film, he wanted to suck my face. Dandering home through the town afterwards, he would put his arm round me and pull me into an alley for another snogging session. I nearly died once when Sandra Jackson walked past with her friend Tracy on their way home from Youth Outreach.

Then we'd stop outside the housing executive and look at the houses for sale.

"We'd have to take out a mortgage to be able to afford any of these houses," he'd say. He was hoping we could open a joint bank account.

Of course, I know now what was wrong with Jonathan. He was a gentleman, he couldn't get passionate unless he also got committed. Jonathan asked the first time he touched my naked breast. Then we sat the rest of the evening in my front room watching television with my mother. "Yes, Mrs French," No, Mrs French, "Three bags full, Mrs French."

My mother was convinced that the sun shone out of his eyes ("what a nice boy") and told me that our "minor relationship difficulties" were my fault. I only said, that though romantic dinners at *The Rainbow's End* were very nice sometimes, they were like red roses – you tired of them after a while.

"Mummy," I wanted to say, "it would be easier to find a virgin in a maternity ward than find excitement with Jonathan."

But I said nothing.

Jonathan said things like, "A levels and boyfriends are a volcanic combination, Mrs French. I don't want to alarm Marian but the next three and a half months are going to be the toughest of her life. And the pressure is only starting to build."

I was grateful that somebody was committed to my A levels. My interpretation of studying was to slog hard till the cup of coffee was drunk and the packet of Hob Nobs finished and then hightail it over to Andersons to eat cake like a fat little piggie and watch scary films on their video. And have really deep meaningful chats with Lynette about discos and clothes and all that. Already I knew that I wouldn't suffer more than one or two mother-induced panic attacks before the exams, but the panic would stem from fear of failing and having to stay in Magherafelt with her. It wasn't perfectionist, ambitious, self-motivating, healthy panic.

I don't think Sonia's panic was perfectionist,

ambitious, self-motivating or healthy either. She was never satisfied unless she was playing all the hardest games and wanted to study veterinary science. The manic energy she'd channelled into catching Paddy Butler at Christmas was diverted into physics, chemistry, biology and maths once the Christmas trees came down in January.

I don't think it's healthy to scratch beneath the surface of people's intentions. Ugly things jump at you. Sonia was not an animal lover, she couldn't have directed you to the milking parlour or the lambing sheds on the farm. But if she wanted to rise at 6 every morning to read organic chemistry and practise differentiation, I, for one, was not going to attach any psychological significance to it.

Sonia's manic panic was making everyone's life a misery. She'd always restricted her psychotic outbursts to the Anderson household before but now her tendency to crack up was filtering through on to the hockey pitch. At one hockey match against Dalriada, the right inner kept shoving her every time she got the ball. One time she even held her arm and pulled her back. Sonia lost the head and hit her full whack on the shin with her hockey stick.

Brave and courageous Ms Dart sent her off. She was lucky Sonia didn't wrap the stick around her neck.

The hockey-playing brain intrigues me. I think the mentality is best suited to the army or the church. Strong on discipline and light on individuality.

"Maybe you'd rather be a games teacher than a vet," I suggested.

She laughed. "Marian," she said, "those who can, do. Those who can't, teach."

She was so worried about her maths A level in particular she studied for it coming home from matches instead of singing "She'll be Coming Round The Mountain When She Comes" at the back of the bus.

I tried again to help. "I was at youth presbytery," I said, "and the talk was about whether God has one plan for our lives, or if there are a dozen things we can do with His blessing."

"So?" said Sonia so aggressively that I hadn't the heart to suggest that maybe veterinary science wasn't the thing for her.

I silently watched her manic exhibitionism with a mixture of irritation and admiration instead. I was such a dull fat sausage compared to her.

"Jonathan says he doesn't want to alarm me but the next three and a half months are going to be the toughest of my life," I told Lynette sadly.

"He says the pressure is only starting to build. So he's not coming home this weekend because a couple of boys in accountancy class have caught the measles and he's afraid that he might smit me. He spent yesterday in bed with a sore stomach, and he's afraid that might be the start of it, or maybe he's just pulled a muscle."

"It's not just that you don't feel very nice," Jonathan had said on the 'phone, "it's the way you don't have your mother to tuck you into bed and fill your hot-water bottle, and tell you not to eat bananas because they're hard to digest and to force-feed you custard instead. You just lie in an anonymous bedroom and feel sorry for yourself."

"Bloody hell," said Lynette, fascinated, "he really is a bit of a Wendy, isn't he, Marian?"

"Not all the time," I said loyally, "he played a sex psychology game with me last weekend when he was home. I'll call Sonia, shall I, and do it on her?"

"I wouldn't bother," said Lynette. "No one's allowed in the kitchen when Miss High and Mighty is battling with her books. And she better not be disturbed until 4.21 because then she'll have done seven hours exactly from when she rose this morning. I personally think that it will be just as important to the world that I know which carbonates fizz with which acids, and Darren knows what the study of the earth's crust is called, even though we learn in freezing bedrooms."

"Come into the sitting room and play *Scrabble* with me while you're waiting. Sonia sits in the kitchen to be close to the food. It's just as well she does so much exercise or she'd be as fat as you, Marian."

"I think everybody's the same when they're studying," I sighed. Lynette was only ever blunt, never cruel. "I used to try to do sit-ups when I felt hungry, but at the rate I was going, I'd never have passed an exam."

"She doesn't have to do four A levels," said Lynette, determined not to be fair. "Nobody is making her be a vet. Our Sonia can't cope with pressure. The peer pressures of junior school are every bit as terrible as that of A level students. Mr Sterling gave us a talk yesterday about adolescence and how he hated it and how he sympathised with the pressures we're under."

"Do you have a notion of Mr Sterling?" I asked her kindly.

"No way," she said. "He made me sit beside Johnboy Jackson in biology."

"Come here and sit beside Lynette," said Mr Sterling.

"I'm all right where I am, thanks," said Johnboy.

"What," says Mr Sterling, "you don't want to sit beside a lovely pretty girl? In a few year's time you'll be swooning over her and you'll kick yourself."

So Johnboy had no choice but to sit beside her.

"It's dead annoying," said Lynette, "and he's annoyed me ever since. Boys are nothing but a nuisance. If they weren't biologically necessary for procreation, girls would have nothing to do with them."

"Even Jimmy?"

"Jimmy Fingers is a red-hot smoocher," said Lynette. "When we swop spit my head spins."

"I thought you were a 'Look But Don't Touch' person," I said.

At 4.21, Lynette was cheating with "Vrates" which she claimed to be curtain material, when Sonia came bursting into the sitting-room. She grabbed Lynette by her ponytail and started to beat her round the head.

"You wore my good wine-coloured jumper last night, you sneaky thing," she shouted, "and you threw it back into the wardrobe with toothpaste all over it."

"Wartface, wartface," screamed Lynette because Sonia had a worrying stress-induced wart at the end of her nose.

She wasn't a bit pleased when I suggested that it was heaven-sent to guard against the sin of vanity. Sonia could dish it out but she couldn't take it. It wasn't really Lynette's fault that she screamed unreasonably about everything. She inherited it from Sonia, who wasn't much of an example. They couldn't stand each other because they were so alike. It was no big deal. It just made me grateful that I didn't have a sister.

"Don't you dare be so cheeky," screamed Sonia, "you're just jealous."

Sonia had a habit of saying, "You're just jealous."

"Of what?"

Sonia started to cry. When stuck for a smart answer, Sonia always cried.

Once they were both crying, I intervened.

"Think of a body of water, Sonia," I said brightly.

Sonia let go of Lynette's ear. It was no wonder Lynette had such odd ears, the way Sonia swung on them.

"Puddle," she said.

"Give me three words to describe it."

Sonia said "wet", "bothersome" and "shallow."

"Jonathan says that 'water' is the psychological term for 'sex'," I said, "so you must therefore consider sex to be 'wet, bothersome, and shallow.'"

"What did you say, Marian?" she asked me, unconvinced.

"Marian said, 'A paddling pool: addictive, uninhibited and adventurous,'" said Lynette, laughing. "Our Marian got an A in her English O level because she learned all the sexual connotations in *Death of a Naturalist*."

"What's your idea of happiness?" I asked Sonia, because I could see her about to retreat back to her books. I'd been granted twenty-seven minutes. By the time she was seated in the kitchen again the half-hour's brain rest would be up.

She smiled suddenly like the cat who got the cream. "Going to the pictures and snogging Paddy Butler."

"And you, Lynette?" I was almost afraid to ask.

"Going to the pictures and snogging Jimmy Fingers."

So there definitely was something wrong with me.

And both Anderson ladies were Guests of Rugby Boys. I was madly jealous.

"I've studied for three hours almost today," I said, rising to leave, "and I couldn't tell you what subject it was."

"Don't let it bother you," said Lynette cheerfully. "I sat and read *Petals In The Wind* all morning instead of *The Silent People*".

"I've studied for seven hours," said boastful Sonia. And she loved snogging her boyfriend in the pictures.

"Jonathan says it's terribly important to find a time of day when you can study your best," I said in my nasty rat-in-a-drain voice. "He says that not everyone succeeds by rising at six every morning the six months before the exams start."

The Andersons were maniacs. There was nothing wrong with me that I preferred watching television or eating to snogging Jonathan in the pictures. The rest of the time he acted like we were forty. I wanted to be swept off my feet. By a rugby boy. Call him Paddy Butler for the sake of argument.

Paddy Butler and I were always in the middle of a passionate clinch. We were meant to be, it was just one of those things; never wanted anybody but each other. I lay in bed at night kissing the inside of my upper arm (the most erotic part of my body that I could reach), imagining him arriving downstairs to declare himself, carrying honeysuckle, daisies or buttercups. I was tired of Jonathan's shop-bought hothouse efforts.

My rugby boy fantasies weren't stories, nothing actually happened in them. They were a series of snapshots threaded with Paddy and me, unshakeably in love with each other.

Paddy and I dressed for dinner at *The Rainbow's End* (suddenly gone upmarket but the Bimbo Sisters still gawking and Big Shirley suddenly obsequious). We smiled across a candlelit table at each other, toes touching beneath it.

Waiting for Paddy at an airport arrivals lounge, seeing him before he sees me watching him search the crowd for me. The joy and pain on his face when he sweeps me into his arms.

Paddy and I hand in hand in the supermarket, throwing smoked salmon and caviar into the basket. Meeting two Gorgons. Donna's hair is greasy and Lisa has lost her figure and they're both pushing screaming brats in prams. Donna Gorgon's husband has left her for another woman and Lisa Gorgon isn't married.

Their trolley is full of sliced pan loaves and bags of frozen chips.

They stare at us open-mouthed.

"Marian French."

"You can call me Mrs Butler."

Paddy writing to me, "You're always in my heart."

And my ultimate fantasy, the one that gave me virgin orgasms. Standing on the touchline at a rugby match in a huge fur coat with his watch on my arm beside my watch shouting, "Women weaken legs, darling."

I don't think it's healthy to scratch beneath the surface of people's intentions. Ugly things jump at you. Paddy Butler was a prat, an alcoholic and smoke-aholic.

"Surely Sonia can see that herself and Paddy Butler are a one-way trip to nowhere?" my mother kept nagging as if it was her problem. "They'd make her turn if she married him."

"I'm sure Sonia would be touched if she knew you were concerned for her welfare," I said calmly. "But she only likes the one of them, not the entire Fenian boy species."

A little voice which sounded unpleasantly like my Christian Conscience suggested that my fantasies were unhealthy, and diagnosed an inferiority complex, living in the shadow of Sonia Star.

I didn't listen. Fantasies were clean healthy fun and, in all the best ones, the heroine found her handsome prince in the end.

chapter six

Exam fever crept silently into the sixth form centre. One day Sonia was reading the *Argos* catalogue and screaming at the junior hockey teams for incompetent Indian dribbling, the next she was sweating blood over physics multiple choice papers at the back of the study room. Some silent whistle seemed to have blown and even Jimmy Fingers responded. He stopped bouncing Lynette on his knee at the back of Room 4 at lunch-time and painted, "Panic Now And Avoid the End-of-term Rush" with a spray gun on the wall of the sixth form centre. Fingers's only other claim to fame in sixth year was creating a "masterpiece of abstract art" (his words, not mine). He piled all the chairs and tables in a huge bonfire format in the centre of the room and called it "Erection".

He was suspended for both creative endeavours. Mr Tweed said he had "abused the privileges of the sixth form centre."

"What does Lynette see in that alien?" Sonia asked for the umpteenth time. "She used to have sense."

"Oh, I don't know," I said, "He's a plonker but I can't help liking him at a distance, the poor lonely header."

But there was something seriously wrong with Fingers. He was refusing to conform to the school code of studying. He was taking a rebellious stand against convention. And after "Erection" he tried to save us from ourselves.

"Marian," he said, "If you let me copy your French essay I'll tell you your fortune."

Like I said, I liked the poor lonely header so I humoured him and held out my hand.

"Primary school," he said. "Grammar school, steady boyfriend, university, engaged, teacher training, married, mortgage, nine-to-five job, Spain for a fortnight every summer, 2.4 kids, childminder, your kids start primary school and the whole thing starts over again."

At the time I said, "I'd rather go to Greece on holiday, Jimmy," but I could see what he was getting at. My bum was going to get very flabby, sitting at a desk all day, pushing paper five days a week, fifty weeks of the year, for forty years. Maybe I was a security addict, like he said.

Jimmy said he believed in predestination even though it was a Catholic idea. "Protestants believe in free will because it's harder," he said. "It means you can't blame anybody for bad exam results except yourself."

"Last night," said Sonia, "Jimmy came up to visit Lynette and he drove past the house about a dozen times before he had the nerve to stop, in case my mother would see him. Hardly surprising when he drives a Lada."

"And what did your mother say?"

"She said, 'What an ugly boy' to me and, 'I'm sure Jimmy doesn't want to see the inside of the bedrooms' to Lynette. Then the little brat went off gallivanting to the *Kentucky* in Ballymena with him and he told her there were three types of woman in the world; the ones for whom plastic surgery would make no difference, the ones that a bit of make-up helps, and the few like herself who don't need make-up to enhance their looks. Then he took her to the carpark in Magherafelt. It's the 'in' place to be, according to Lynette, the cars fly round and it's packed."

"I'd nearly go out with Fingers myself if he was going to pay me compliments," I said.

"Well, you missed your chance there," said Sonia and we both laughed.

Jimmy felt that the sixth form should contribute to society and stop bleeding it. He said students were all "Take, take, take." So he organised an interview with Mr Tweed.

"A sponsored bed push," said Mr Tweed. He didn't even look up from his desk at us. Jonathan said people did that when they wanted to feel superior to other people. If you don't look at someone when you're talking to them, you aren't giving them any signals, so they don't know where they stand with you. In a normal conversation, you look at the person when you start talking to them, then you look away and, when you're about to stop talking, you look back at them.

"What charity is it for?" said Mr Tweed briskly, "Have you a route? How long will it take for the average team to go round the route? Is the route outside the school grounds? Have you asked the police for permission? What's the timetabling like? Will runs have to be done at night? If so, what provisions will be laid on and will it be sixth formers who do the night runs? Have you asked members of staff for assistance? Are you aware of the large-scale disruption it would cause to teaching time?"

Mr Tweed was worried about Jimmy's attitude problem. He was worried that Jimmy would incite the rest of us to rebellion. In assembly, Mr Tweed gave us pep talks about exam pressure and pacing ourselves and peaking at the right time. But it never occurred to us to break the chain and shout, "Stop the world, I want to get off." The Protestant work ethic says, "It's better to achieve through application than inspiration."

Sonia whispered, "Jimmy, your zip's down," in the middle of it.

"Well, all right then," said Fingers. "Will we have a sponsored onion-eating event instead?"

"Jimmy," I suggested after the interview, "aren't you madly excited by the prospect of university? Do you not think Magherafelt is the most claustrophobic town on earth? Don't you appreciate that we're only studying and conforming and being girlie swots so we can escape from here?"

Jimmy laughed at me.

"You'll have to go further than Belfast to lose your small town mentality, Marian," he said.

I had a wonderful fantasy about student life. It would be my metamorphosis. I would live in a bedsit at the top of a delightful old house, my rooms would be tastefully decorated and my mother would never come in to snoop around. I'd wear eccentric clothes, like painter's overalls, and I'd be very small and thin and my hair would be long and shiny. When I emerged, with a wonderful degree, four years later I would be a different person, reinvented. Jonathan never invaded this fantasy, but one time Paddy Butler came to the door when I was wearing a towel and asked me if he could have a cup of sugar. I chased him. I would not have a crush on Paddy Butler when I was a student.

In the end Jimmy organised an "End of the Mocks" disco in the rugby club with all the proceeds going to charity. On a Thursday night, which meant no Jonathan. Mega till I discovered a rugby old boys dinner at *The Rainbow's End* the same night.

"If you take Thursday night off, you'll have to work Sunday instead," said Big Shirley when I asked her. She really had it in for me sometimes. She bossed and bossed until my head was turned, even though I often spent hours on my hands and knees scraping out the inside of ovens with a Brillo pad. I never had enough money, so I always volunteered for all the jobs going, no matter how dirty. Even though it meant I had to make up stewing time at the weekends and on holidays. I even studied on Sundays, though that was disguised as "novel reading" (of English and French literature course work) in my mind.

I often fantasised about the day when I would walk out of *The Rainbow's End* for the last time. The day when I wouldn't have to skivvy to make ends meet.

It was all right for Sonia. She only worked when she felt like it. Big Shirley complained of her lack of commitment and Sonia told her to stuff her stupid job. That was the difference between Sonia and me. She had the confidence to say it and I didn't. But then Sonia didn't need the job and I did.

It was easy for Sonia to advise that I dump the last of the whipped cream that I'd overwhipped into butter. "Hide it and she'll never know," said Sonia. She didn't have a Christian Conscience to pester her into confessing every naughty thing she did.

"You're so selfish," Sonia said once. "Offloading your guilt on other people and making them carry your burdens."

"Shirley," I said, "you know I don't like working more than one Sunday in the month."

Shirley's eyebrows shot up. "If the Bimbo Sisters can work more than one Sunday in the month, then why can't you?"

I felt blue, not my usual bouncy self at all, crabbit even. I had a mad urge to snap at her and bite her nose right off. Sustained stints at *The Rainbow's End* were doing nothing for my mood. The Bimbo Sisters were Catholics. It was a religion I was unfamiliar with. But, as far as I knew, so long as they went to Mass on Sunday, they were free to sin as much as they liked the rest of the afternoon. Unlike us Presbyterians.

"It's against my religious beliefs," I said lamely.

"Are you good-living, Marian?" she said. "I'd never have guessed."

She had no heart. It was a conclusion I had reached ages before, a sad revelation. Where had her heart gone? Was it stolen by some man who had refused to marry her?

One of the Bimbo Sisters said she had been engaged once to a tight-fisted accountant called Roger Moffett, but he dumped her at the altar. Apparently he'd told her not to be wasting her wedding savings on a fancy wedding dress and to wear her mother's and use the money to buy a three-piece suite instead. And Big Shirley had disobeyed him and turned up to the church in an extravagant affair flown in from Paris that morning, and Roger had taken cold feet and jilted her.

"Of course," said the Bimbo Sister, "she hasn't been right since."

Big Shirley suddenly smiled. "I'm in foul form today," she said, "so don't take it personally. You'd be doing me a massive favour if you went on stand-by on Thursday night, just in case I need you."

"What," I said sarcastically, "like *Top Gun?*"

Lynette was also having problems getting to the disco.

"Mummy," she said, "everyone, and I repeat, everyone who isn't a social recluse, like Sandra 'Bible Thumper' Jackson, is going to the rugby club on Thursday night. Anyone who is anyone in the school will be there. Even all the nerdy boys aren't missing it. Even the third years are supporting it."

"Yes, darling, I know," said Mrs Anderson vaguely. "Sounds like marvellous fun. Might pop in myself for a bop with Jimmy."

"You're not going, Lynette," said Sonia sullenly. "The last time you went to a rugby disco you made an ass of yourself facing Jimmy Fingers up against a wall. It was really obvious you were desperate for a man."

"What I love about you," said Lynette, "is the way you're so nasty to my face. Most bitches are nice to your face and a cow behind your back. I'm tired of being treated like a stupid baby, Mummy.

"All I'm allowed to do is go to school every day, do homework and study, sit in on a Saturday night and sing like an angel in the church choir on Sunday. What sort of an existence is that?

"Look at me," she shouted, "Coming out of school today I was in the world's best mood. I got A's in all my mocks. Now I'm sickened."

"It does sound dull," said Mrs Anderson. "You must be the dullest girl in the whole school, Lynette. If you're not careful, Jimmy'll trade you for a faster model."

"I've even got the outfit," screamed Lynette. "My first ever little black dress came in the post this morning and Marian is lending me her girdle so I bought the ten and not the twelve. I'll be paying that dress off, 99 p a week for the next thirty-two weeks of my life. The O levels will be over and I'll still be all dressed up with nowhere to go."

"All right, all right," Sonia sighed resignedly. "I'll take you. Anything for a quiet life. But you'll be overdressed and stupid-looking in the black dress, Lynette. It's a rugby disco you're going to, not the Oscars. Don't say I didn't warn you if everyone laughs at you."

Lynette smiled. She was famous for her quick smiles. They were usually so brief you missed them.

"Thank you, darling Sonia," she cooed. "I'll remember you said that the night I'm getting an Oscar."

I two-timed Jonathan at the after-the-mocks disco.

I'd spent quite a while on my appearance. In my opinion anyway I looked marvellous. The mocks were over, I was excited and ecstatic and all that.

"If Jonathan phones," I instructed my mother, "tell him I'm out. Flames die down sometimes, Mummy, and we were too warm anyway."

"That wrapover top thing shows your spare tyre," said bitchy Sonia, who was letting her cardigan fall provocatively off her shoulder. She was a real pain sometimes. But she must have noticed how well I was looking. If I hadn't been competition for her, Sonia wouldn't have commented. Paddy wasn't coming. He was studying. "Treating her mean, keeping her keen."

We weren't in the door five minutes when I saw him. Standing with his big macho mates. Pitter-patter. My heart nearly stopped.

"Cor blimey," I whispered to Lynette, "I could really fancy him."

"I thought," said Lynette, "that you were Marian 'oh so serious' French, the girl who was destined to die a virgin?"

"Fat chance." I grinned.

She looked him over. "I wouldn't kick him out of the bed for eating toast," she said. "But he's not worth two-timing Jimmy for. Even Jimmy in those jeans. No harm to him, but they're the worst I've ever seen him in. Not that I'd ever tell him in case I hurt his feelings."

Lynette had done an hour's housework for her mother to earn a pound to hire Sonia's Christmas dance black lace gloves for the evening. "I'll be watching you like a hawk," said Lynette, "and so will the rest of the school."

He had an adorable big grin and I asked him to dance. I wasn't feeling a bit like Marian "oh so serious" French that night. It was "French Kiss" with all the gross heavy breathing. I didn't care. Everyone thought I was a strait-laced goody-goody, hooked on security. It was driving me mad. For once in my life I wanted to seduce a boy for the crack of it.

One minute we were dancing energetically, the next we were holding hands, then sweetly and innocently we kissed each other – touch that for romance if you can!

He was clutching my arm when he bought me a drink – a sure sign that he wanted to get closer.

As we headed for a snog in a nearby chair, I saw Sonia out of the corner of my eye, and her mouth was hanging open. The rest of the night we sat with our arms round each other, real cool. I waved at the Gorgons who were dirty-looking me. He was nice, he respected me and didn't grope like some boys. He was sexy and gorgeous.

"You're in for some great times as a free agent," said Sonia on the way home. "Are you going to see him again?"

"What do you think I am, desperate?" I said.

"What are you going to tell Jonathan?"

What indeed.

Jonathan borrowed his mummy's Metro to take me out to dinner to celebrate the mocks being over. When he saw me he grabbed me and made me kiss him. I was nearly sick.

"I missed you so much last night I did fifty sit-ups, and a pile of press-ups and I'd have run ten miles if I'd had a pair of training shoes to run in," he said.

I felt a bit miserable about the situation. If I didn't confess to him some other wee sneak was bound to tell him. Sonia had been surprisingly supportive.

"Let them bitch," she advised. "Who cares?"

You know, sometimes she was all right. She wasn't always a nasty bitch who didn't think I was good enough for her, and who thought the sun shone out of Paddy Butler's nostrils.

"If anybody calls you a slut, I'll kill them," she said.

Should I concoct some elaborate excuse? Would he jump down my throat? Would he finish with me? I'd been for a long walk, to think about the situation, and I didn't have any answers. I'd even cried a bit, out of self-pity.

Was he going to spend the night moaning about student grants and dingy accommodation, and how he had to carry his underwear home to Mrs Lamb to wash at the weekend?

"I made a cheesecake out of a packet last night," said Jonathan cheerfully as we ordered at *The Rainbow's End*, "and I didn't throw up so it must have been OK. How did the disco go? Did Sonia two-time Paddy Butler?"

He was making me feel like a prize asshole. Guilt was

eating me up. He had such a trusting, kind face, and I realised bitterly that I was still addicted to security.

"The men were after her in swarms," I said. "I was bored out of my brain because everyone was stone-drunk. And I two-timed you."

As Sonia would have said, I only said it to make him feel bad. So he would take away my guiltiness.

But I hadn't bargained with Jonathan. Jonathan started to cry.

chapter seven

Jonathan changed. Maybe it was the weather after Easter, spring and all that. He phoned to tell me he'd joined the parachute society at Queen's.

"The man says that when you jump, if your reserve parachute fails, you're to cross your legs because it makes it easier to unscrew you from the ground."

Then he added that he'd got my letter and carried it about with him all day, not close to his heart but in his trouser pocket ("and you know what that's close to, Marian").

Was this the boy who asked the first time he touched my naked breast? Would I be safe with him ever again? I decided to ask Sonia and the world was indeed a desperate place when you resorted to Sonia Anderson for advice. "It sounds like he's finally turned into a man," she said. "He'll be calling you Miss Garden Path next, like Paddy calls me. He says I lead men up the garden path and then, when they're about to open the gate, I shut it in their faces."

"Well, it's better than being called Super Dog," I said,

"like Mandy Gorgon is." We were in biology and it was boring because Ms Dart had come to visit Mr Sterling again so the boys had a "Design Something Else For a Tampon To Do" competition, and "Frank Bruno, World Heavyweight Boxing Tampon" won. One time Paddy pierced his ear with a safety pin in class.

Sonia and I were trying to place an adjective to everyone:

Jonathan Lamb : Cuddly

Paddy Butler : Hairy.

"And put Super Dog underneath for Mandy Gorgon," said Sonia. "She gets right up my nose sometimes, the way she tries to steal other girls' boyfriends."

Bravely said. Everybody knew that Paddy Butler was sniffing round Mandy Gorgon.

"Paddy Butler is a slag," said Lynette, but nobody else talked about it or, if they did, they made sure Sonia didn't hear them. It wasn't only Lynette who had been on the receiving end of Sonia's hockey stick in the past.

She was still so much in love with him that she didn't even blow herself kisses in the mirror in the morning.

Sonia shrugged at my Jonathan problem. "I would advise you to deflower him," she said, "providing you take precautions. Look what happened my mother."

Yes, indeed. Mrs Anderson had pulled a fast one on all of us.

Jimmy Fingers was snogging Lynette in the back seat of the Lada on Good Friday night and she tapped the car window and said, "Sorry to be a bore, Jimmy. Would you mind dropping me off at the hospital on your way home? I think I'm having a baby."

I don't know how she managed it. Since Neil died, I hadn't seen Mr Anderson once. He wouldn't have recognised me if we'd met on the street. Sonia said he spent most of his time gallivanting round the country at sheep sales. Maybe it's only a fantasy that a family disaster brings couples together. Perhaps it depends more on the couple involved. If they can talk, they'll pull through together. But if you're married to the strong silent type, you're left up shit creek without a paddle.

They called the baby Neil which I thought was very sinister. Reincarnation was the last resort if you couldn't accept a death, I thought. But I was only a raw adolescent, and the greatest pains I'd experienced were cosmetic ones. Every time I looked at the bald infant I imagined the other Neil in a rugby jersey with an adorable grin.

"Would she have called the baby Neil if it was a girl?" I asked Sonia.

Sonia shrugged. She refused to talk about her new brother. My mother said it was because he put her nose out of joint.

"It was very inconsiderate of her to drop it just before my A levels," she said. "And if it's a new hobby, I hope she tires of it soon. Every time I see her she has him attached to her breast. And don't give me that crap about breast being best, Marian, that you read in the biology textbook. She could breast-feed him discreetly."

"Well if your mother can make mistakes with the facts of life, I'm keeping my legs crossed," I said but she wasn't listening.

I took my books to Belfast, to study when I visited Jonathan. But I read the *Christians in a Sex-Mad Society* book on the way up on the bus – they didn't advocate anything more exciting than kissing. I tried to study my Helena Curtis biology textbook but was such a bundle of nerves the reproduction section went in one ear and out the other.

Jonathan met me in Belfast with a red rose. I did not feel weak with emotion when he kissed me, which worried me somewhat. In fact I felt pretty sick, but reading on the bus might have caused that. How could such a platonic feeling last forever? I was obsessed with "forever". Either I was frigid, as Sonia had suggested (no wonder I didn't like her), or Jonathan and I weren't meant for each other.

His house on Surrey Street (pronounced Slurry Street) was embarrassingly dirty and frightfully cold – what was my mother thinking of to let me stay up there on a Friday night? But of course she trusted Jonathan. He was like a second son to her, she said.

There were wine bottles ranged along the fireplace (which gaped like an empty eye socket). Jonathan didn't drink, of course. He was a member of the Tea Towel Club (Send six tea towels to six friends, etc. and in six weeks you'll have thirty-six tea towels). I was so nervous I chattered nineteen to the dozen the whole way from the bus stop. Lynette Anderson and I had made six pounds between us, selling daffodils at the Thursday market, and our hands were destroyed from pulling them; Wear Your Own Clothes Day at school had been nothing but a fashion parade; *The Rainbow's End* was nothing but a load of slave labour.

In the end he pulled off one of my socks and stuffed it down my throat. We romped around on the living-room sofa for a couple of hours (the housemates having gone to the pub; probably we should have gone with them – the pub that night was the lesser of the evils). Once I warmed up, I started to enjoy myself too much. He was kissing me all over and I was feeling dizzy and delirious even though I was still wearing all my clothes. Such sweet and tender passion. Lying back and letting it all happen. If the male's sex drive really was ten times higher than the female's I might have caused him to have an accident.

"Jonathan," I begged weakly, "go and take a cold shower, you're making me nervous."

"Frigid Brigid." He kissed my hair. "You have a curve at the base of your spine, you're soft and warm, you have eyes full of promise." But he got off me. I might not be so lucky the next time.

God, I prayed quickly. Help me, my flesh is too weak to help myself. I mean, there I was on the bus to Belfast thinking Jonathan and I were a lost cause, he irritates me, he's a Mummy's boy and now I can't drag myself off him for the sake of decency. He is exploring me and I'm enjoying it.

"What's the difference between an erection and

leaving the light on?" Jonathan asked when we were walking down the street to the Freshers' ball. "You can sleep with the light on," he said, but the cold air (it was the windiest, rainiest, rudest night I could ever remember) had cooled my ardour and I briskly said, "You should never confuse lust with love, Jonathan. I'll sleep on the floor in a sleeping bag. Out of harm's way."

"Don't do that." He was desperate, disappointed. "I've been waiting for weeks to get you on my own."

"I bet you have," I muttered, slapping spotcream on my shoulders and dabbing some *Anais Anais* into my cleavage. "What man wouldn't mind a woman in bed with him? I hope my Christian Conscience isn't going to kick up a fuss about me sleeping beside him."

It was my first experience of sharing a bed with a man and I didn't enjoy sleeping beside him at all. He breathed loudly when he wasn't snoring. And every time I turned away from him, or complained of the heat, he suggested I take my pyjamas off. What had got into him? I endured it until twenty past four. There were still cars driving up and down Slurry Street. I wondered where they were coming from and where they were going. In the end I got out of bed and slept on the floor. I felt like a bit of a dog but I couldn't bear the noise around me.

Next morning Jonathan made me breakfast in bed, branflakes and toast, and got into bed beside me while I ate it. He was wearing a penis happy head.

"Don't eat too much," he joked, "my flatmates will be suspicious."

But the flatmates were drunkards and hadn't surfaced

at noon when we strolled into town. We bought chocolate-covered mint fudge (it cost 50p a quarter pound) and ate it together. Jonathan asked the Bard of Belfast (resident outside *Primark*) to recite "Making Love In Áras an Uachtaráin" (Jonathan had one thing on his mind and it wasn't poetry). I did one of those *Test Your Sex Appeal* games and got "Too Hot to Handle", which delighted him because he was sure I would be a demanding lover (even if he had to wait till the wedding ring to find out). He whispered sweet nothings in my ear all day but I said I felt sick, and didn't appreciate them.

Actually everything he did irritated me. He kept saying things like "Why don't you buy some sexy lingerie for me?" We fought on the way home.

My mother was regretting her bohemian approval of my visit. Once Jonathan had unstuck himself and gone home she did the Sex Talk – "It's very easy to get pregnant," and all that. A bit offended and a bit guilty, I said I wasn't interest in having sexual intercourse (or "making love" to quote Jonathan). Then she got worried and demanded an explanation of such a nun-like remark. Sometimes there's no reasoning with mothers.

chapter eight

D-Day approached. The study room was packed when Sonia was dragged screaming to her physics practicals exam. It was a day when I had eight free periods and I was unfortunate enough to land beside Jimmy Fingers. In the six hours we were there I don't think he did more than twenty minutes work.

He talked instead. "Marian," he said, "did you read in the paper about the girl in Omagh who killed herself worrying about her O levels?"

"Is this a tasteless joke?" I whispered.

"No, she was so wound up she couldn't get a breath and after she was dead the doctors diagnosed anxiety."

The story sent a goose galloping over my grave.

"Pity she hadn't heard of the theory of reward," Jimmy mused. "The girl who couldn't catch a breath."

Jimmy had hired a sunbed for the duration of his exams. It was installed like a canopy over Lynette's bed and he lay under it to relax and unwind in the evenings after a hard day distracting the faithful.

One of the Golden Rules states, "You catch more flies with honey than with vinegar", so when he started to peel an orange I sweetly told him I was allergic to them – anything to get rid of him – and he went outside to eat it in the boys' toilets.

When he left, Mandy Gorgon offered me a sweet from her stack. There didn't seem to be any strings attached and I was dumbfounded. Maybe she wasn't such a cow after all. But you never knew where you stood with her. She was like the snake in Reverend Robinson's sermon one Sunday. The snake asked a little boy to carry him across a river. The little boy had been told that snakes would bite you if you went near them. But he lifted the snake and carried it across the river anyway. And when he set it down on the ground, the snake bit him.

"Jimmy's a bit of an oddball, isn't he?" Mandy whispered.

"Hard to handle," I agreed cautiously as Sonia came in. Mandy was the most consumer-friendly of the three Gorgons and was often used as the infiltrator, lulling her victims into a false sense of security until they blabbed. She had a great gift for acting like a human being when she wanted to.

Another minute and I'd have been telling her about Jimmy's sunbed and the way he posed naked on it for Lynette to practise sketching her still life for her art O level.

"Sonia even looks brainy," said Mandy, "doesn't she?"

"I'm absolutely ripping," said Sonia loudly. "I couldn't

get the light spot on the ballistic galvanometer to move. Furious does not describe my mood."

"So how is our arrogant genius?" said Jimmy, who'd come in the door behind her, and she elbowed him in the kidneys. He almost collapsed in agony and half the boys in the study room squirmed and crossed their legs.

"Gosh, Jimmy, I'm really sorry she got you in the kidneys," I said when he was taking me home in his Lada in payment for a loan of my study notes. "You might never have been able to regulate the osmotic potential of your body again."

"She's good crack," he said, "I don't mind her being snappy. It's fun. The Andersons are the only girls I know who aren't all sugar and spice. I'd be bored out of my brain without them. Playing *Monopoly* with Lynette is like World War 3. She was premenstrual all week, and last night she had the worst period pains in the whole world. She couldn't sit up and she couldn't lie down. She was almost vomiting. I had to walk her round and round and make her hot drinks and rub her belly and read *The Silent People* to her. I even taught her to burp to take her mind off the pain. The wee pet has her first English exam tomorrow afternoon."

What sort of boy was Jimmy Fingers that he could talk about menstruation and not make a dirty joke about it?

"Reproduction fascinates me," said Jimmy. "Not only women either. Look at oysters, Marian. How do you know which is a boy and which is a girl by looking at them? How do they know themselves? So how do they mate with each other?"

In a half-hearted attempt to knuckle down to study, I'd removed the revolting lace curtains from my bedroom window and shifted my desk so I could look out on the street.

My mother came in with a glass of milk and a Fifteen bun when I was listening to *Kaleidoscope*. "It's for the biology paper tomorrow," I said. "They're discussing the *Kama Sutra*, and they're not even laughing."

I was as fascinated by reproduction as Jimmy. Maybe everybody is at seventeen. But my interest was definitely focused on male reproduction rather than on oysters.

"I suppose it's pre-exam nerves," said my mother. "Put that lace curtain back when it passes."

To be fair to her, my mother tried very hard to be normal during my Λ levels. Maybe she'd also heard of the Omagh O level suicide. Or maybe she was as terrified as me that I might fail all ahead of me and be forced to remain in Magherafelt with her.

Sonia phoned about six o'clock. "I've started to cheer up," she said. "Maybe the light spot on the galvanometer moved after all. And there were two magpies in the garden when I got home from school, two for joy. There's no point worrying myself into a frazzle thinking I've failed. Everybody can't fail and I'm brighter than most of them. Half the class think the light didn't move on the galvanometer either."

"It's not like you to behave like a rational human being in the face of imminent disaster, Sonia," I said, half joking. "Have you been drinking?"

"Better than that," said Sonia. "Paddy and I are

playing squash together tonight." Silly me to forget the essential ingredient in Sonia's mental make-up. Factor X.

"Will you always go running when Paddy Butler clicks his fingers, Sonia?" I only asked out of curiosity.

"Oh, yes," said Sonia seriously. "In case he doesn't ask me a second time." I met them later on in Magherafelt main street *en route* to my baby-sitting job at Reverend Robinson's. Sonia was sitting on the crossbar of Paddy's bike and, when she saw me, she waved and shouted "Marian!" Paddy swerved into a litter bin and knocked her off on her head. He wasn't a very brave person for all his bluff. He walked on down the street with his head held high, whistling *A Bicycle Made for Two*.

"Did you ever see such a pathetic attempt at bum fluff?" he said as he passed me, pointing back at Sonia's French plaits. She was still on the road, rubbing her elbow and examining a hole in the knee of her new pink track suit. "And tell her not to take the track suit off again, Marian, T-shirt and shorts doesn't compliment her figure. She's like a breakfast, two fried eggs, and her legs are like matchsticks."

I said "Have you forgotten to shave, Paddy, or is that a pathetic attempt at bum fluff on your chin?"

"What a pity I wasn't comatose," said Sonia cheerfully. "It would be dead exciting to be in a coma in the hospital, with Paddy washing my face with his tears."

I thought it was only me who fantasised about such things. Her lovely track suit was covered with bike oil.

"He has a great body," she informed me as I dusted her

down. "And our squash together is terrific. Such satisfaction. I'm definitely still sexually interested, even if the spiritual and mental bits need a bit more polish."

They'd met a couple of rugby old boys when they were coming off the squash courts.

Rugby Boy 1 : "Hi, Paddy. Who's this lovely lady?"

Paddy : "Grunt."

Rugby Boy 2 : "Off for a bit of sex, are you, Paddy?"

Paddy : "Grunt."

"I wanted to curl up and die," said Sonia. "In the space of ten seconds I was depressed, then furious, then vengeful. I'd have wrapped my hockey stick round his dangly bits if I'd had it with me. But I blew my top instead and shouted at him and told him to piss off, I never wanted to see him again."

"Love works in mysterious ways," I said, groping around for something pleasantly clichéd to say, "And the path of true love never runs straight, Sonia. Half the time Paddy Butler talks to have something to say. Communication is a two-way process."

"Exactly," said Sonia. "He knows that I'm mad about him and he treats me like dirt. But pig that he is, I think even he realised that he'd pushed me too far. So he groped my bum, and said, 'Typically girlie of you to take it so thick, Sonia.' That's about as close as I'll ever get to an apology from him."

Sonia wasn't a low-IQ individual. It was just that if Paddy had been a yes-man like Jonathan she wouldn't have spat on him.

"I've news for you," said Sonia. "Guess who my

mother spied in the maternity wing of the hospital this afternoon wearing a new size sixteen track suit?"

"Ms Dart!"

"Ms Dart?" I said. "But how can she be pregnant? She's not even married."

"You better read your biology textbook before the first paper tomorrow, Marian," said Sonia laughing.

I babysat for Reverend Robinson, our new minister, for one reason only. I hoped God would notice and swing a miracle for me in my A levels. So I didn't even bother taking my books with me to study. Instead I read the dreadful little Robinsons bedtime stories as practice for teacher training. It didn't take a careers officer to advise me against primary school teaching.

Isaac pointed at my spots and asked, "What's those red things on your face?"

My spots were cystic and boil-like along my jawbone but Sonia had diagnosed frustration, not exam pressure. She said I needed a man.

"I have Jonathan," I pointed out.

"I said a man," she said.

She was probably right. But it didn't make me feel any better, nor did it remove the disfigurement.

Unhappily I ate the Reverend's pâté, drank his orange juice, his coffee and milk and nibbled his chocolate wholewheat biscuits.

"I'll not take payment," I said when it was over, "providing you pray for me." But Reverend Robinson said his prayers were free and gave me a fiver anyway. When I was leaving he said, "I wouldn't place undue emphasis on prayer, Marian. God helps those who help themselves."

My mother reassured me that all children weren't as hyperactive and noisy and cheeky as Isaac Robinson.

She said that if the new Reverend and his wife spent less time gallivanting off to clerical dos, and more time with the little Robinsons, they might acquire some social skills and not be such wee brats.

"The sacrifices I made for you," she joked. I think it was a joke anyway.

To further assist with my biology first paper preparations, I insisted that Jonathan escort me to the sexually perverted film at the late night pictures. It was the French film, *Betty Blue* and I told Mummy it was to help with my French conversation exam. I secretly hoped it would also help with my biology.

"Well, I wouldn't kill to see that film again," Jonathan said when we were leaving. "It was a bit dirty in parts, wasn't it?"

"It's purely for educational purposes," I said. "I now feel completely confident of full marks in my French conversation and any sexual reproduction questions on the biology paper."

"You only had to ask," said Jonathan, "and I would have given you a peek."

We had discussed having a "mutual trial separation" until my exams were over.

A mutual trial separation meant that Jonathan wouldn't take me out anywhere, and I wouldn't go out with anyone else. Enforced fidelity. It didn't quite rank with Indian wives flinging themselves on their husbands' funeral pyres but it wasn't an open relationship either.

"Everyone thinks we're 'heavily involved' anyway," I said. Heavily involved meant that he phoned me every night, though the conversations were packed with pauses.

I gave him a tonguing once when he phoned at the start of the *Eastenders* omnibus, and told him straight that he was losing his sparkle and in the background I heard his mother yelling, "You're under the thumb, Jonathan."

"Forget about my feelings," said Jonathan nobly. "Do what you have to do." And of course I didn't do anything and nothing changed. I was still Big Marian, the dull fat girl, so starved of glamour that any persistent man, be he Chinese, Malaysian, Pygmy or Irish Fenian could have swept me off my feet. I was afraid that I'd never be asked out again.

As Jimmy had so charmingly phrased it, "I see you as a female," he'd said kindly, "a non-gender friend."

I didn't think that that was a compliment. It was no wonder I stuck with Jonathan since other men saw me as a sexless counterpart.

I just didn't have the nerve to finish with him.

"Men have no intuition," Sonia told me when I confessed as much to her, "He'll never guess." But she did give me one piece of sage advice. "Take a good long forenoon," she preached. "For the afternoon might be exceedingly tedious with him, Marian."

A see-through male penis was the first diagram on the biology paper. I had to laugh. I was still laughing when there was a commotion at the back of the hall. Lynette Anderson made a grand entrance, smiling at everyone. Mr Sterling followed hard at her heels. I heard Sonia swear behind me. She would never have mistaken a morning exam for an afternoon one.

"Do you not think I acted cool?" Lynette said afterwards. "I was lying on the sunbed when Mr Sterling phoned. What else could I do but smile at you? And all of you 'as stupid-looking as bloody bullocks.' That was the only quote I could remember from *The Silent People*. The essays were really stupid and I didn't have time to check them over, but they weren't what I'd planned to revise this morning anyway."

"My exam was diabolical," said Sonia loudly, "wasn't it, Marian? I hadn't a clue. The paper was absolutely awful. I'll be relieved if I get a 'C'. Nothing I prepared came up. My face must have been a picture when I looked at the paper and couldn't answer any of the questions. I was so desperate I even prayed."

"Should we go and see Mr Sterling?" I said. "It was Mr Sterling ruined my concentration before the exam," Sonia snapped.

"I popped into his office to ask him about aggression but he was that busy being monopolised by Ms Dart that all he could say was 'Aggression, has that to do with your hockey training, Sonia?' And the old slapper noticed that I forgot to put my tie on when I dressed this morning. My head was so full of vital information that I couldn't shake it in case some fell out."

"Didn't do you much good," said Lynette spitefully. "I

noticed you looking round you and picking the hairs off your blazer. And you were the only person to leave half an hour early."

Things were hotting up nicely for a sisterly slanging match.

I gave Sonia a pamphlet once on temper control but it irritated her so much she ate it.

chapter nine

Mr Sterling organised a treasure hunt and barbecue at the port for sixth form to celebrate the end of our exams. We planned to stay in Sonia's caravan and my mother would only let me go provided Jonathan came with me.

"But I thought you didn't trust me alone with Jonathan," I protested.

She shrugged. "When I stand at the Judgement Bar on Judgement Day I don't want to admit to letting my seventeen-year-old daughter go to the port for the night on her own," she said. "Better the devil you know, Marian."

Tears and pleadings never worked in our house. I'd tried sulking before. I'd tried impressing them with stewing for my exams. Nothing worked. Sometimes my parents could be an obnoxious pair of cretins, and some days they gave in without a fight.

It wasn't that I didn't want Jonathan there, but this was a sixth form party and he wasn't invited. Even Jimmy Fingers was going without Lynette. He raced past us in his Lada with Paddy firing a water pistol from the passenger seat window. Ever-competitive Sonia put her foot to the floor to catch up.

Jonathan was stroking my hand in the back seat which I found quite irritating, though of course I didn't say anything. He put his arms round me as the Vauxhall Nova began to shake. "I don't want you to be in a car crash," he whispered, but he didn't tell Sonia to slow down.

Afterwards, on the beach, everyone teased Sonia because Lynette had won all her races on school sports day and broke all the junior records. She even won the Open 1500 m, beating Stephanie Bruce, captain of the senior cross-country team. And she won it after falling a clatter at the start (people said afterwards that Stephanie had tripped her).

Paddy started to laugh. He said, "Sonia Star didn't enter in case her wee sister beat her."

Sonia's huffy attitude problem got the better of her and she flung herself on Paddy with a very credible rugby tackle and wrestled him to the ground. Jonathan said that the rugby boys were convinced he was just using her. I didn't know what to think or where to look. They snogged for an hour under Paddy's anorak, oblivious to the surroundings and the tons of food. I confess I was taking more than a passing interest in the seduction. I noticed them going for a walk at about half one with their arms around each other.

Once we'd eaten our fiver's worth, Jonathan and I slipped into the sandhills for a pretty passionate snogging session ourselves.

Sonia had diagnosed my irritability as sexual frustration, so up there in the sandhills I seduced the poor boy and almost drove him to frenzied passion (naughty, eh?). Jonathan said he thought he could go the whole way given half a chance, but his logical thinking wouldn't let him. Thank God for logical thinking.

But as I was going to France for the summer to stay with a French family and perfect my accent for university French (God willing), I could afford to be generous before I left.

My Christian Conscience said it wasn't fair to keep Jonathan hanging on waiting for me to fall in love with him when I was desperate to spread my wings.

But I'd started to outgrow my Christian Conscience at that stage and didn't waste my time listening.

I'd saved £100 spending money, waitressing at every bus tour tea and wedding reception in *The Rainbow's End* since Easter.

"I feel really pleased because I earned every penny of it by the sweat of my brow," I told Sonia the evening before I left.

"*Merde,*" said Sonia rudely. She had a camp bed positioned inside the back door and was basking in the afternoon sun. It was too cold to lie outside. Sonia was jealous because she was spending the summer trailing after the vet on "seeing practice" before she entered vet college in the autumn (God willing).

No one dared suggest Sonia mightn't get the necessary As in all four A levels to get to vet college. It was a subject all of us were sweeping neatly under the carpet.

"Have you heard," asked Sonia, "that Alec Sterling is getting married in August? He told me that when we were wading through the answers to the biology third paper. I bet he's got some wee doll pregnant and has to marry her."

Usually people like myself live tedious, humdrum lives where nothing exciting happens and things are never very high nor very low.

The morning I was due to go to France I was fantastically organised. I'd packed my bags into Sonia's Nova the night before. It was a mother's place to take me to the airport, but my mother wasn't a conventional mother. She'd paid for the flights provided we could have a series of running battles monthly, during her PMT week, when she would criticise the quality of my French accent. Then she took me shopping the week before I left and bought me a pile of expensive sunblocks, to prevent skin cancer. She bought me a good pair of wine-coloured sunglasses for an astronomical £9.50. "If you sit on these and break them, I'll never buy you another pair," she said.

"What time is your flight leaving?" my mother asked on the appointed morning, in an effort to appear interested.

"Ten-fifteen," I said.

She frowned. "Are you sure you're booked on the quarter past ten flight, Marian?" she said.

"Of course I am, Mummy," I snapped impatiently, but I checked the ticket anyway to please her. The flight went out at half nine.

"Oh no," I said. "The flight goes out at half nine."

My mother started to titter. "How could you have been so stupid?" (Answers on a postcard please.)

"Mummy," I pleaded desperately, "will you drive me to the airport in the two-litre Ford Sierra? It would be faster."

I never asked my mother for anything. But I was desperate that day.

"Sorry, dear," said my mother. "There isn't enough petrol in it, and there wouldn't be time to stop for a refill. And anyway I'm scared of crashing it."

So Sonia and I bundled into the Nova to race for the plane (with one breakneck emergency stop for me to run back in for my tickets).

I felt seasick with the lurching as Sonia pumped her foot on and off the accelerator. There were roadworks on the M2, traffic lights in Antrim, two lorries and a tractor with slurry tanker on the last couple of miles to the airport, and a yarning policeman when we got there.

We double-parked on yellow lines and made a run for it. Even now I remember Sonia screaming at the girl behind the desk, "We got here at twenty-five past nine, why won't you let her on? I'll become a bloody security risk if you don't let her on that plane!" I led her away before the men in white coats came to get her. She was screaming about writing letters to *The Times* and flying by the rival company in the future.

"We burst through Security," she wailed. "We pounded up the escalator walkway thing. We elbowed our way through bovine travellers, and we got to the desk at 9.25 am. And they wouldn't let you board. If you'd been a well-fed business man in a suit and tie, or a rich bitch in flashy clothes, I bet they would have let you on."

Hockey training, or no hockey training, her heart was still coming up her throat. The only redemption was that my mother had forked out the full whack – only the best, we Frenches didn't fly on the cheap, it was tempting fate or something – so I was able to get the 10.15 flight after all.

It was OK. It was irritating and tiresome but hardly a life-or-death situation (Sonia even phoned home to tell my mother that I'd caught the flight. Very important to keep up appearances).

"You know," said Sonia, when I'd got her a cup of tea and people had stopped pointing at us, "these might be the last few days of mediocrity in our lives. In a few years time, I'll be rich and beautiful and famous and married and flying in the clouds. Like the pair impressing each other beside us."

We turned round to look at them.

"I just love South Africa," said one. "I go there to read."

"I just love the toilet," Sonia mimicked. "I go there to read. And you'll be a very bored Mrs Lamb, and you can come and visit me."

My French family were probably not bad people – but they were such a bad influence I even went shopping with them to *La Grande Motte* on the Sabbath, and bought a jumping spider. It was to scare off the real spiders in the bathroom. I don't have a phobia about spiders or anything, but one had been hiding in my towel and got squashed on my face when I was drying myself, which was a bit of botheration.

The battle-axe mother, Cruella de Ville, was most certainly psycho, but more the Mrs Anderson school of madness than my mother – "The knife is more deadly than the tongue." One day on the beach the temperature reached 44°C (three people died, but not on that particular beach). I was distinctively clad in size fourteen shorts that I'd bought in Top Shop – which were too tight on me – a peaked cap and the new sunglasses.

We'd only been on the beach an hour. Already my underarms smelt like poison-gas. After I'd arrived I discovered I'd brought two pairs of bikini bottoms and no tops. Isabelle said, "There is no problem, Marian, everyone is topless in France." She suggested it was the hypoallergenic total block sun cream I was lathering on that was making me smell. I stuck to my shorts and T-shirt (literally) and let Cruella and Isabelle form their own opinions of the eccentric British.

"Cruella," I said eventually, "I'm going to the café."

Cruella said, "Wait for Isabelle, she'll go with you." A kind thought but Isabelle, (the de Ville frogspawn), was at that point flaunting her body to the male population and had no wish to waste time with boring pink me.

So I ambled off up the beach to the café where I drank eight various items to quench my thirst and told myself that such spending was going to have to stop. I ordered a couple of sandwiches as well and got the eye from a real

Frenchman. He had really dirty fingernails but he looked like a cross between Omar Sharif and Roy Orbison. My mother says French men go really mad for fair spotty damsels. Something she didn't tell me was that the French didn't eat in the middle of the day, and then they ate really late at night. I was so hungry by then I got indigestion.

I returned to the de Ville beach party feeling decidedly desirable and sexy. Cruella imperiously beckoned me over and began a great French scolding, something about it not being very jolly to waltz off to the café seule. Wearing a bewildered and inane look, I diligently tried to follow the French but as Cruella didn't speak it with a Ballymena accent (à la Mr Tweed) the dialect differences made translation difficult.

On the Saturday night before departure we went to a beach party. I hoped I would grow up to look like beautiful, elegant Cruella who wore a different glamorous swimsuit to the beach every day. That night she was immaculate and elegant in white trousers as she danced with Monsieur de Ville (also in white trousers) to "Wonderful Tonight." I certainly didn't want to be like Mr and Mrs La Bamba who were dancing beside them. They had drunk too much and had a row on the dance floor because one of them was whirling in the wrong direction.

I couldn't believe how much I enjoyed myself. Boys actually asked me to dance. None of them were as good-looking as Isabelle's flavour of the minute, Fabrico. So I took a photograph of him to take back to show Sonia and make her jealous. He was a screw.

Cruella had a French hangover the next day and began accusing me of not speaking enough French, and not helping enough around the house (a lie; cleaning is not my strong point but I'd tried to remember to wash my lemonade glass).

"You do nothing but read books," she screamed. (This was justified. I'd brought *Pilgrim's Progress* and *From Witchcraft To Christ* with me for spiritual guidance. But I read four blockbusters instead, each of them at least two inches thick.) I hadn't even had a summer romance. Isabelle attracted all the men without trying.

I suppose I was glad to be home. Jonathan was waiting for me. He asked me if I was willing to fight to make "us" work.

Privately I didn't think I was. The French boys had gone to my head.

But what was the alternative? Find another boyfriend? Face him a couple of times and have it fizzle out after a couple of weeks? Then I would have nobody. I was only eighteen but in our society, unless you had a man attached, no one took you seriously. I have an aunt who reads the news for BBC television in London but, when she comes home for weddings and things, my mother never asks her about her apartment in the West End or the designer clothes or the exotic holidays. First question is always if she's found herself a husband yet. "That's what happens to educated women, Marian. Your aunt Angela went the whole way to London and got herself a job at the BBC and she still couldn't catch a husband."

I told Jonathan I wanted us to try again.

Then I phoned Sonia.

"Sonia," I said, "I waited for your letters in France with bated breath, and I choked. Why didn't you write to me?"

Sonia sounded depressed. She said something catty like, "Is your tan almost visible this year, then?"

It was Mr Tweed, the careers officer, who suggested she spend the summer with a real vet before going to vet college (God willing). So she wasted valuable man-eating time riding shotgun with Mr Pym (a fossil-like specimen who got one out of ten for attractiveness, and that was only his car).

"The only bit of excitement I got was when his car broke down and Paddy Butler, large as life and still a bollocks, was working in the garage where it got fixed," she told me. "He was earning £5 a day to fix lawnmowers and he was wearing black-and-white trousers that were the worst I'd ever seen. We might not be an item any longer, but the view's still better from the shelf."

I hadn't expected her to ask me how my summer went so I just listened to her talking about herself.

"The rest of the time I endured endless mastitis in dairy cows and let's face it, Marian, when you've felt one hard tit, you've felt them all; I held a dozen tomcats getting their testicles cut out; I sewed up ruptured pigs; I stood out of the line of fire of a racehorse with scour and I worried about my A levels."

And tomorrow we were getting the results. No wonder she was being so nasty.

"I had a ghastly nightmare last night," she said. "I dreamed I got 16% in my maths. Lynette says it was caused by eating two fillets of mackerel, two hunks of bread and cheese, and a piece of apple tart before bed. And it's not a premonition of what's to come."

Sometimes I think there should be self-help groups for people who believe in omens and read their horoscope, and believe them. Before she hung up, Sonia said she was a bit worried because Saturn was in her Aquarius and she could imagine him there belching, farting and scratching and herself having to hoover round him.

"If I do fail them all," she threatened, "I really will start believing God has deserted me instead of putting it on to scare you, Marian."

I felt ill with anticipation. "We'll go together tomorrow," I offered," and hold each other's hands."

I think you treat people the way they expect to be treated. Jonathan expects to be walked over, Jimmy Fingers expects to be ridiculed, Sonia expects me to sympathise with every emotion she suffers, but have no feelings myself. So I spent the night tossing and fretting about her A level results and not about my own. You couldn't tell Sonia that the course of her destiny would not be determined by the grade she got in her maths A level. She wouldn't have believed you.

Sonia was manic the next morning but it wasn't just A levels causing it. She'd just heard that Mr Sterling was marrying Ms Dart. Shock. Shock.

"Do you know where he's taking her on honeymoon? They're going to Pluket. It sounds like an ideal honeymoon destination, except the dirty deed has already been done."

"Please, Sonia," I said, thinking, "there but for the Grace of God go I."

"Apparently she's going to change her name to Mrs Sterling after she's married," said Sonia. "So much for the feminist Ms. Of course, maybe he's taking her away there in the hope that he'll get rid of her. Did you read that thing in the papers about the man who went on holiday to south east Asia and came home with no kidneys? He got drunk on his last night there and he died on the plane on the way home and they discovered that he'd had his kidneys removed. There's a big market for kidneys, you know."

Sonia got four Es in her A levels. I looked at the results slip and she looked at it again and started to laugh. Not hysterically, not even maniacally. With relief.

"Now I don't have to be a vet," she said. "Now I can be anything I want."

part two

chapter ten

Sonia left Paddy Butler after three years of emotionally turbulent marriage.

"She was impossible to live with," said Paddy, "she broke the heads off all the flowers the day she left."

I felt very sad for her, of course I did, but I also felt cynical. Why do people insist on marrying the first bit of Grand Passion that comes their way? Love-hate relationships are not happy marriage material. You should only get married because you want to be married, not because you think you can't live without the loved one. What usually happens is that you realise, after a couple of rollercoaster rough-and-tumble years, that you can't live with him either.

Enough of the preaching. Jonathan Lamb and I have been saving to get married for three years now. When we got engaged, Jonathan bought my ring in a jeweller's offering a "Free Meal For Two and Free Ring Insurance for One Year" engagement ring package. Maybe I would have preferred an emerald crusher like Sonia's but the free meal offer only extended to diamond solitaires. At our free meal for two, I waited until Jonathan had eaten every scrap of his Chicken Kiev and I said, "Can we concentrate on the financial aspects of our union for a minute, darling?" Jonathan was learning to be an accountant. His eyes lit up at the words "financial aspects".

I said, "I don't think we should rush into marriage just yet, Jonathan. We can't afford to. There isn't enough money, not with your mortgage and our two cars to pay off. I don't mind waiting till we can afford two hundred guests, six bridesmaids and a honeymoon in the Caribbean."

Jonathan finished chewing and thought for a moment. "But, sweetheart," he said, "wedding days are only one day in our whole lives together. It would be foolish to squander money on a fancy dress and an exotic honeymoon when we could be saving for a rainy day."

Jimmy Fingers's fortune-telling prophecy was progressively coming true. I lived at home and taught English and French in the High School. Jonathan had a mortgage on a house in Belfast. We'd been to Cyprus twice on holiday. Then we get married . . .

All my life I'd been waiting to get married. To be a beautiful bride, to float to the front of a packed church on my proud Daddy's arm, to reassure a stunned bridegroom that the vision of loveliness was really his Marian . . .

So what was holding me back?

When Sonia married Paddy Butler it was a sad sordid ten-minute affair in a grubby registry office.

Mrs Anderson was very miffed about it. "This is very selfish of you, Sonia," she said the morning of the wedding, "You could have converted and had an arch of hockey sticks at the chapel door. I may never get the chance again to see the inside of a Catholic church. You're no fun any more."

"If you were any sort of a mother at all," said Sonia irritably, "you'd have disowned me for marrying a Catholic. Like Marian's mother would have done."

One of my mother's most famous statements was: "If you marry a Catholic, Marian, I'll say 'Marian? I have no daughter called Marian.'"

"Well, how boring," said Mrs Anderson. "When being the bride's mother is nearly as much fun as being the bride. Marian, darling, when you're taking the photographs, try to remember that the left is my best side."

The Anderson family circus. Some things never change. Mrs Butler made a speech at the booze-up back at the house. "They say opposites attract. I don't agree. I think that if two people like themselves, then they're going to like someone with the same traits that they like in themselves. I love my husband because I see myself in him."

Lynette whispered, "Do you know why they got married in such a hurry, Marian?"

"She's pregnant?" I said.

"Of course not," said Lynette, "not even our Sonia's

that stupid. She was afraid Paddy would change his mind again. Nine days out of ten, Paddy has nine other girlfriends."

"And on the tenth day Sonia caught him," I said.

And after three years of emotionally turbulent marriage she left him.

"Madam is upstairs in bed," said Mrs Anderson when I arrived at the farm," making everyone's life a misery."

"How is she?" I said.

Mrs Anderson waved a manicured hand. "She's eating and drinking so there can't be much wrong with her," she said.

"You're looking well," I said nervously to Sonia. I always said the wrong thing.

Sonia sat up in bed. "Tears must be good for the complexion," she said.

I twisted my diamond solitaire. "Maybe it's just a storm in a teacup," I said. "You and Paddy are both headstrong and passionate people. It's always the bravest person who makes the first move towards reconciliation."

Sonia and Paddy were always having bust-ups when we were at school. Give or take a couple of times she hadn't told me about, she walked out on him on average twice every month. It was just Sonia's little way. To make a crisis out of a drama.

"You think I'm making a crisis out of a drama again, don't you?" said Sonia bitterly. "You and my mother. She came in earlier to ask me would I be staying to dinner or should she pack me a lunch for the bus journey back to Belfast."

"So you've really left him this time?" I said stupidly.

"It's been building up for a long time." Sonia sighed. "I kept waking up at night and crying and crying and bursting into tears in the middle of the day. And then Lynette came to visit me and we went into town for a girlie session because she said an expensive facial and a bottle of vodka would cheer me up. She's just found herself a new boyfriend and she was so mega happy I felt even more miserable. And then I felt jealous of her. And then I felt guilty for feeling jealous of her. And then Paddy came home from work with lipstick on his collar again and I decided enough was enough. Do you know what he said when I was trampling the flower-beds? He said, 'But you know I'm a bachelor boy, Sonia.' He thinks I'm having another psychotic tantrum. But I'm not. It's all over," she said importantly, "and I feel sick."

"Stop," I said. "Sonia, you've got depression. Having depression is not a reason to leave your husband when he's never left you because of it."

Give Butler his dues. He was a B category man, who would always have six girlfriends on the go at once. Sonia knew that when she met him and when she married him. If he hadn't been a B category man she'd have said it was a monotonous relationship. Jonathan always thought her obsessive interest in Paddy Butler was unnatural.

"She's clever, articulate and sporty," he said. "She could have gone anywhere, done anything, been anybody. But she married Paddy Butler and he wasn't even faithful to her on their wedding night."

I shrugged. "It must be very tedious," I said, "to be clever, articulate and sporty all the time. Something's got to give." I thought they were ideally suited. There aren't many men who will tidy the house after their wife wrecks it, and stand by with a box of hankies to mop up the inevitable tears which round off a psychotic tantrum. Compromise is the secret of happy marriages. Nobody was wearing rose-coloured glasses the day Paddy and Sonia became man and wife.

"Well, I'm not going to say that it's all for the best," I told Sonia, "because I think that's the most empty comfort anyone can give. I will say one thing though. It could be worse. You might have had to come home to my mother."

It was a difficult time in my mother's life. Stephen had finished four years at Queen's University and turned into a lazy poof. He mumbled constantly, which was driving me mad, and he was always scrounging money and never said "thank you" when I gave it to him. And when he was asked to do something, like go outside for the coal bucket, he whinged and bitched so much about "discrimination" that I wanted to shake him and do it myself.

"I knew this would happen," said my mother. "I said he should have been a plumber."

It became her mission in life to find Stephen a job. All summer he lay in bed listening to Bon Jovi, and my mother bought newspapers and visited job centres and filled in application forms and forged Stephen's signature because he'd grown too lazy to write his own name.

The day he got an interview for the civil service in Belfast, she combed his hair, chose his tie, polished his shoes and drove him there herself in the two-litre Ford Sierra.

"Stephen," she said, "are you listening? I wrote on the application form that you play rugby for the Old Boys, and that you were head boy at school, and the secretary of the computer society at Queen's."

"Yes, Mother," mumbled Stephen. He shambled so slowly into the interview, I think lice were jumping off him.

"Have you set the date for the wedding yet?" she asked me as we sat in the car waiting for him. She asked this on average twice a day.

"No, Mother," I said. "But I promise you'll be the first to know when we do."

"A long engagement is a bad thing," said my mother briskly. "Your granny used to say 'Something might pop up.'"

A short engagement is a bad thing too, I think. If Sonia hadn't thrown caution to the winds and married Paddy Butler on a whim, on a day when he was in the mood for commitment . . .

"I had Lynette in to speak to my first year English class yesterday," I said.

"What did she talk to them about?" asked Sonia nastily. Lynette Anderson is a bit of a superstar in Magherafelt. You could say she has put us on the map. She doesn't read the news, it's even better than that.

She's a journalist. A really mega famous journalist. She writes for a pile of really posh magazines. And she's only twenty-five. Makes you sick.

"Now, Sonia," I said severely, "you know as well as I do that people queue up for Lynette's creative writing workshops. It was a very great honour for us to have her last year. And this year she inspired Nicola Gorgon to produce half a page on the physical charms of Brad Pitt."

There are a hundred things worse in the world than unmarried pregnancy. But I believe it was poetic justice that Mandy Gorgon, Super Dog caught it. Machiavellian Mandy, who ingratiated herself with me during our A levels. She'd been secretly pregnant through the whole of it. She joined the push-chair brigade in the autumn. I went to university and Sonia went to sixth form college to repeat her A levels. Nicola Gorgon is the most foul-mouthed child I have ever taught.

"What do you read?" Lynette, the creative writing superstar, asked Nicola Gorgon.

"I can't read," said the belligerent brat, "I just look at the pictures."

Lynette smiled sweetly, her professional smile, not her real one, and turned her back on Nicola Gorgon. We had an educational psychologist teach us about disruptive influences in the classroom when I was at teacher training and I remember him advising stuff like drawing a circle of chalk on the floor and making the child stand in it. When Lynette turned her back on Nicola Gorgon she did the same thing, figuratively speaking. She talked about partying and rave with the rest of the girls and said, "I'm giving you twenty minutes to write me a page about boyfriends while Miss French makes me a cup of tea."

"That skitter at the front," she said quietly to me, "she reminds me of somebody."

Nicola Gorgon was the last to read her story.

"I'm not reading it," she said sullenly. "Don't have to read it if I don't want to."

"Of course you don't," said Lynette, smiling again. "But no one is leaving the room till you do read. Make us another cup of tea, will you, Miss French, while I lock the door and throw away the key."

"She's Mandy Gorgon's daughter," I said, "the one that shifted your brother Neil the night he was killed."

"Hmm," said Lynette, "that would account for her guttersnipe character, but not for her features. How discreet of Mandy Gorgon to keep the father's name a secret."

"I don't think she knows who the father is herself," I suggested.

Finally Nicola Gorgon read.

"I'm only reading because I have to go to the toilet," she said.

Sonia laughed and laughed when I told her the story. Sonia and I are poles apart in a lot of things but a pathological interest in the Gorgons is a common bond that we'll carry together to the grave. One Gorgon down, two to go.

No matter how hysterical Sonia got, she could always laugh at a dirty joke.

"I think one passionate love-hate relationship is enough in any lifetime," she said.

chapter eleven

I've always said Lynette Anderson had more brains than any of us. When she was in upper sixth she wrote a fashion report of our school speech day. I keep a signed copy pinned to my bedroom wall.

It starts, "A prestigious social event. In silence, honoured pupils marched to their seats. Hair is smoother and more geometrical this year. Only one unruly bob of poodle curls was visible. Make-up was very subtle, no accessories. Colours this year are red, black and white, fabrics cotton, polyester and wool. A 'Back to School' group of designs with skirts knee-length, shoes heavy, legs muscular to carry them . . ."

I suppose anybody might have written it in a moment of idle boredom. But Lynette wasn't satisfied with simply writing it. She decided to enter it in the writing section of Elle talent contest as well.

"I'm sure winning these things is all psychology," she told me. "Glamorous magazines want young, good-looking writers. If I had multiple chins and varicose veins they wouldn't want to know me. Beautiful people have easier lives."

The solution, Jimmy Fingers decided, was a professional photograph.

Jimmy, as it happened, dabbled in photography. His studio was a damp garage that smelt of cat pee. I'd never been there before but was enlisted as "photographer's assistant" for the shoot since the regular assistant, Lynette, was the "subject".

"Don't touch anything, Marian," said Jimmy. "Most of the equipment isn't paid for yet."

"What will I do, Jimmy?" I enquired politely. There was a certificate on the wall – Jimmy Fingers had an A level in photography.

"Well, of course I do everything," said Jimmy importantly, "but you could make the subject a cup of tea, please, Marian, while I put her at her ease. This takes away the self-consciousness of posing. Lynette has a nervous mouth, you know."

I sat on the high stool while he rummaged through lenses and filters and things and studied me through the camera.

"You have a very interesting face, Marian," he said. "That's what we photographers tell the subject when she isn't pretty."

The subject appeared from the dressing-room looking dead glamorous with her hair pinned up and her make-up on.

Jimmy frowned.

"Lynette, pet," he said, "your hair looks like spiders' legs growing out of your head."

"Piss off, Jimmy," said Lynette comfortably.

While they argued, I crouched beneath the high stool holding a light-reflector board.

Eventually a compromise was reached. The photograph was fabulous because Jimmy had, through luck, I suspect, not talent, captured Lynette's real smile, the one that was so fast you usually missed it.

She sent the fashion report and the photograph off to *Elle* and together they won. A star was born.

The *Elle* talent competition had a photography section as well and Jimmy entered a couple of photographs of my "interesting" face. That was a long time ago but I can still recall the disappointment on his face when they were returned in a stamped addressed envelope of appropriate size with a stiff little note that started, "We regret to inform you . . ."

"They called it 'literature'," Lynette said when she came home from the prize-giving in London. "They said, 'You couldn't learn to write the way you write, dear'. I was really flattered, of course, but I didn't believe a word they said. And they're going to put my photograph into *Elle* too, and I think that's far more important than my fashion report because nobody will be bothered reading the fashion report but everybody will see the photograph. I think I'm going to enjoy being famous if it's all about eating big feeds and meeting people. And having congratulations showered on me."

Fame rarely comes without its problems. Jimmy Fingers was the first casualty.

"My girlfriend is famous," he'd say. "You can look but you can't touch."

Page three boyfriends probably go on the same way. Jimmy made loads of jokes about locking Lynette away till she'd written enough to pay the rent and he spoke knowledgeably about the poverty-stricken appearance of artists reflecting their "feast-famine" existence. But his heart wasn't in it.

I never suspected Jimmy's aspirations to stardom, I thought he took photographs and played his guitar in a band for fun.

Two big egos is one too many in a relationship. Professional jealousy crept rapidly into what had once been a beautiful balance. Jimmy became the Humpty Dumpty who pushed his girlfriend off the wall because he wanted to see her crack.

Lynette's debut performance as a "Writer" was at Ballyronan Festival the week before the Twelfth of July. She was asked to read her prize-winning *Elle* entry on stage, before a sketch by the Young Farmers and after a pile of sad poetry written by a sad woman down our road. The Orange hall was packed because the winner of the best-kept garden was to be announced at the end.

Lynette brought Jimmy and Sonia and me to laugh at the funny bits and clap at the end. She warned us not to clap at the end of the sad poetry, she said we had to sigh loudly instead, because that's what the people in London had done at the prize-giving.

"Didn't I do well?" she said proudly afterwards. "But I'll have to wear flat shoes if I ever do it again. I nearly broke my ankle when my leg started shaking. Thank God I was wearing a skirt and no one could see."

Jimmy didn't say, "You were wonderful 'darling'" or, "You were marvellous," or any of those things she'd brought him along to say. Artists are rare plants full of insecurities and his lack of heartfelt praise (and Jimmy's warm heart was his vital organ) must have disappointed her. When Lynette was seventeen she was utterly convinced that she was in love with Jimmy and, as I'd never had a boyfriend with whom I was in love, I was utterly fascinated by the way it made her feel. It made her very vulnerable. I decided quite quickly that I wouldn't like it. Jonathan Lamb giving and me taking was a more pleasant alternative.

By the time she was twenty, Lynette didn't just write funny stories anymore. If you asked her to write a cartoon for the *Beano*, she did it. If you wanted a political feature for *The Irish Times* you got it. That was, she said, the secret of good journalism.

Her innocent ambitions met their first major roadblock when Reverend Robinson wrote requesting an interview "at her closest convenience". He and Mrs Mulholland were coming "to discuss recent publications".

"Maybe he'd like you to do a piece for the church magazine?" I said hopefully when she showed me the letter. "Maybe Mrs Mulholland is going to offer you a three-article contract or something."

"Maybe he's going to excommunicate her for writing

that blasphemous bit about Bible censorship," said my mother.

Lynette had written a piece for *Shift* magazine entitled *Should Anything Be Censored?* In the article she said that, as she'd had a very religious upbringing and read most of the Bible, she considered herself qualified to advise that the half of it be cut out. There were bits in the Old Testament about Judaic laws and eating pork which weren't applicable nowadays. And there was a completely unsuitable bit about a woman being stoned at a Hebrew well for lifting sticks on the Sabbath which had upset a very dear friend of hers (me) for days because she had a waitressing job in a restaurant on Sundays at the time.

"It's all your fault as usual," said my mother cheerfully, "you and your damned Christian Conscience. I told you it was a luxury you couldn't afford at sixteen."

We gathered in the Anderson house as the appointed hour approached. Sonia said she would crouch outside the open windows of the lounge and take notes. Mrs. Anderson, who had baked scones for the visit, said she was going to hide in the attic because the voices would rise and she might be able to hear better than Sonia. All the family cars were parked round the back of the house in case the Reverend invited us all into the living-room.

Lynette laughed at my nervous face. "He isn't going to ask me to name the friend who had a waitressing job on a Sunday, Marian," she said, "and I very much doubt he'd coming to brand me with 666. But, just in case, I'm going to have a notepad and pen with me and record everything he says – no doubt he will do the talking while Mrs Mulholland pulls the strings. I reckon he'll be so nervous that he'll leave after ten minutes."

She had placed her beautiful professional photograph on the top of the piano for confidence.

"That's still the loveliest photograph of you I've ever seen," I commented, pointing. "She looks just like a younger version of you, Mrs Anderson. but I bet she can't make scones as delicious at these."

One thing about Jonathan Lamb, he taught me how to talk to mothers.

Mrs Anderson giggled like an adolescent. "I tell you," she said, "all that talk about farmhouse cooking is a myth. There must have been a black slave in the kitchen doing all the work. Our mixer has broken and it took me half an hour to beat that cream with a fork."

"That fabulous photo of Lynette is only fabulous because it has been touched up," said Sonia nastily. "Our Lynette's not that fabulously beautiful, nor is she that photogenic."

"You're absolutely right, Sonia," said Lynette laughing, "but my Jimmy can air-brush the plainest face and make it interesting. I'm sure he'd be only delighted to photograph you if you asked him nicely."

"My mother says he's only coming for your own good," I said helpfully. "It's for your spiritual welfare."

Mrs Anderson said, "He who is without sin let him cast the first stone."

I would never understand the Andersons. Lynette was on the verge of eternal damnation and lots of nasty things and Mrs Anderson was making little jokes as if she didn't care. But, as my mother said, Mrs Anderson's conscience was clear. Lynette had claimed in the article that she'd had a very religious upbringing.

"Martin Luther was excommunicated," I said, "but take heart, Lynette. I was reading my Bible before I came over and it was "Judge not, so you will not be judged" followed by that bit about taking the ruddy great plank out of your own eye before you examine the speck of dust in someone else's."

I still played Russian roulette with my Bible readings. I treated the daily selection procedure the way Sonia read her horoscope. If it was good I believed it.

"So I'm shadow-boxing with someone else's hidden motives?" she said. "In that case they'll be getting no tea either."

But it wasn't the censorship piece that had incensed the Reverend and Mrs Mulholland. We should have guessed that neither of them would be reading *Shift* magazine. It was a short story she'd written for *Cosmo* about the morals of country people and how, contrary to popular belief, it was actually easier to get "nookie" in the country than in the town. Anyway, she'd used a few biological terms during it, and taken the Lord's name in vain, and Reverend Robinson had been approached by a number of members of the congregation who were concerned because Lynette Anderson was breaking the Third Commandment. And the "nookie" referred to in the story, what exactly was "nookie"?

I went weak at the knees when I heard this but Lynette was cool as ice.

"Reverend Robinson," she said gently "words like 'breast' and 'penis' are taught in O level biology classes."

Jezebel. Sinner. The girl who wasn't scared to say "breast".

Then Mrs Mulholland elbowed in.

"What's 'nookie' then, young lady?" she demanded. You could have heard her in Magherafelt.

"I assume you had a boyfriend when you were a girl, Mrs Mulholland," Lynette said pleasantly. "And when he left you home from organ practice and the prayer meeting, no doubt he kissed you goodnight. Well, Mrs Mulholland, you got a bit of 'nookie'."

Reverend Robinson was hiding in his chair. Lynette rounded on him.

"So you're a *Cosmo* reader too?" she inquired.

"Oh no," blustered the poor Reverend, "I never buy it and I wish I hadn't seen it this time."

"Didn't Pilate say that?" Lynette asked politely. "Do tell, Reverend Robinson, which bits of my story did you find offensive?"

"Most of it," said the Reverend bravely, "but particularly the bit at the end where you referred to the mating flight of the honey bee as an 'aerial gang-bang'."

"Well," said Lynette, "in future when you find something offensive, Reverend Robinson, I suggest you stop reading at the first naughty word you come across and don't read on to see what happens next."

I hate to satirise such an interview. Mrs Mulholland was the personification of my adolescent Christian Conscience but Reverend Robinson was decidedly out of his depth. He was a simple man who played *Nintendo* games with his daughters and watched the American wrestling with his sons. As they were leaving, Lynette said, "I only take Communion when I feel worthy of it, Reverend Robinson. I hope the rest of your congregation have as clear a conscience as I."

Then she added, "It's the soul afraid of dying that never learns to live, Mrs Mulholland."

Jimmy Fingers took fright after that. Suddenly he realised the enormous implications of being Lynette Anderson's boyfriend. If people were going to point the finger at her, then they were going to point the finger at him too.

Lynette was an artist and a sensitive flower. She couldn't stop writing just because somebody didn't like it.

"If I choose to write about 'sexual intercourse'," she said in the pub afterwards, "I will bloody well write 'sexual intercourse' and not go pussyfooting around it with adolescent innuendoes like 'nookie'."

Lynette Anderson is one of the most upfront, honest and straightforward people I know. She has never said a nasty or underhand thing about anyone in her life. She is one of the few people I've ever met who genuinely believes that "He who is without sin let him cast the first stone." But if she'd been a bit less innocent of the bitchy side of life, she might have weathered the storm better.

That was probably why she let Jimmy go without a fight. He'd been beastly to her for weeks and she ignored it and humoured it the way you apparently do when you're in love and waiting for a rocky patch to pass.

"No," she said cheerfully. "No, Jimmy's not coming to see me tonight, Marian, he's going out for a beer with Johnboy Jackson."

"Again?"

"It's only the eleventh night in a row, Marian, and I saw him for half an hour on Sunday afternoon."

There was on article in Shift once (written by a man) which said that 80% of men were abusers who couldn't permit women into power positions. "Abuse", a much maligned word, could cover anything from wife-beating to withdrawal. Whether he knew it or not, Jimmy Fingers was part of the majority. He was not a man who could carry his wife's handbag with pride. He was a red-blooded closet chauvinist.

And he was always drunk and permanently verbally abusive.

"You really should get something done about your ears," he said, "now you're famous, Lynette. People will laugh when they see them on television."

"You really don't have any breasts at all, do you, Lynette? Your public won't know if you're a girl or a boy when you stand sideways."

Lynette held her chin high.

"It's one of the Golden Rules, Marian," she explained after a particularly vicious attack at a party one night. "In a relationship, you publicly back your partner in everything, even when he's being a bollocks."

But Jimmy went too far with Mandy Gorgon. Even Lynette drew the line at sharing Jimmy with a Gorgon.

Jimmy was belligerent. "You've changed so much in

the last three years," he said. "You aren't the girl I fell in love with."

"Don't take your frustrations out on me, Jimmy," she said. "If you can't cope with me being successful now, you certainly won't be able to cope in the future. And if you can't cope, then you don't really love me. You parade me off in front of your friends and then you resent me for it. I'm not going to apologise for being who I am and what I am."

I didn't really blame Jimmy for backing down when he had the chance. But it only proved what I had always suspected. You could attach as many psychological explanations as you wanted, the bald fact and the bottom line was that he wasn't good enough for her.

chapter twelve

Sonia couldn't stop crying. She was like a bored toddler. The minute you stopped paying her attention, the tears started again.

"Can you find the switch that turns her tears off?" said Mrs Anderson. "She's making a frightful mess of her face."

"My mother expects me to have got over the chore of leaving my husband after three weeks," said Sonia. "Even though she didn't get over Neil dying for months."

"Everyone thinks their own tragedy is the worst ever invented," I said, "and they do say that the break-up of a relationship is the worst kind of suffering next to a death."

"I see you and my mother have been reading the same books again," said Sonia sourly, "and the next bit of comfort you're going to offer is to tell me I have to work my way through the various stages of heartache because putting off the inevitable only prolongs the agony."

"Well, actually, no." I laughed. "You forget that I spend my life sweeping things under the carpet."

Why suffer when you can escape?

"My finger feels bare without his ring," Sonia wailed.

"Get out of bed, Sonia," I said briskly. "I'm taking you shopping."

Sonia sniffed suspiciously.

"Marian," she said, "It's three o'clock on a Saturday afternoon, where do you propose to take me?"

Oh, the dreariness of living in the country. A trip to Belfast is considered a day's excursion and enormous breakfasts are consumed before departure, and sandwiches made for the journey which must take all of twenty minutes up the motorway.

"We're going to Magherafelt," I said firmly, "and you're going to parade up and down the main street until you buy something. Put on a pair of sunglasses and nobody will notice you've been crying."

Sometimes I think I'm turning into my mother, the way I dish out brisk and unsympathetic advice. But not quite. My mother would have said, "You won't need sunglasses, Sonia, there'll be nobody looking at you."

"Decisions, decisions," said Sonia, laughing, in Magherafelt. Half of the shops were still selling summer clothes at discount prices, and the rest had their Christmas stuff in the window. "Will I buy some tinsel or some sunblock?"

We met Nicola Gorgon in *Boots*. She was with a couple of guttersnipe friends. They nudged each other and pointed at us when we passed.

"Some things never change," I said. "It makes me feel quite young again to have a Gorgon picking on me."

Sonia frowned. "Has anyone ever confessed to fathering that spawn?" she asked loudly.

"Popular opinion places the blame on your husband's loins," I said.

"I very much doubt that," said Sonia. "Paddy passed his A level biology, even if Mandy Gorgon didn't."

Operation Entertain Sonia became my full-time job. Once upon a time, when sisters were devoted to each other. Lynette would have leapt on the first plane, train or automobile out of Dublin to support her sister in her hour of need.

Bearing this in mind Sonia telephoned Lynette.

"I know you have a hectic life," she said politely, "but would you mind me coming down for a couple of days in the middle of the week?"

Lynette hummed and hawed. She took a creative writing workshop on Tuesdays, and she was going to the theatre on Wednesday, and there was a dinner party on Thursday, and "what with the set-up here" she really didn't think Sonia could stay, and anyway she'd planned to go to the west for the weekend.

"Would you mind?"

Lynette and her boyfriend had officially moved in together. They were trying to build a relationship. They were at a delicate stage of budding intimacy and the last thing Lynette needed was her wailing sister bearing horror stories of broken love.

The world keeps turning even when gravity pulls some couples apart.

But it is bewildering to be rejected. Bewildering and

sickening. "What has made her like that?" said Sonia, "Just because she's got a boyfriend. Why can't she bear to have anyone visit the love nest? I'm hardly going to steal him away from her, the state I'm in."

"Maybe they make a lot of noise together," I comforted, but I too was bewildered and sickened. Lynette had often gone on holiday with Paddy and Sonia when they were married and she was manless. They'd shared an apartment in Majorca for a fortnight one summer, the three of them.

"Do you think Paddy and I were perverted in some way that we enjoyed her coming with us?" said Sonia.

Lynette had an incredible ability to make an unwanted visitor feel unwelcome and she could be openly hostile to anyone she suspected of coming between her and her man. She had indulged in a succession of little love affairs since Jimmy Fingers took fright five years before. They never lasted very long. The first cohabitation took place in London. I was visiting Aunt Angela when I encountered it. We met for a drink in Covent Garden. I believe I surpassed myself conversation-wise. Lynette sat on the loved one's knee with her back to me and they talked to each other about friends they had and I didn't know. I ignored it, the way I had already ignored the way they kept me hanging around waiting for them for an hour and a half, and assumed I was even more boring company in London than I was in Ireland.

Sonia had had an even worse experience. She'd gone to stay with them for a week and Lynette had forgotten she was coming. "Paddy Butler might be a bastard," said Sonia, "but at least he has the manners to make people feel welcome."

They hadn't helped Sonia with her bag, they hadn't even offered her a cup of tea. She had to ask if they minded if she made herself a bit of toast.

"How long are you going to be here for?" asked Lynette.

You learn by your mistakes. The men changed but the symptoms were always the same. Lynette was best visited between them.

I decided to take Sonia to Donegal for the weekend.

"The *Gemini* Hotel," I said. "It has a sports complex and a swimming-pool and there's free entry into one of the nightclubs in town. We can go and strut our funky stuff like old times. Just the two of us. It's my treat."

Jonathan would never guess if I borrowed a couple of hundred from the wedding account. He hadn't been his jovial self in a while and I needed cheering up as much as Sonia.

"You've got fat, Marian," he said when I refused again to set a wedding date. And he persistently lay on my breast and squashed it when we were having a bit of nookie on his living-room floor.

"Is your biological clock ticking away?" he asked.

In the end I'd risen, pulled down my vest, and gone home.

So escaping to Donegal for the weekend was as much Operation Entertain Marian as anything. It's common knowledge. The boys from Donegal know how to show a girl a good time.

When Sonia opened her mouth to protest I said, "A friend in need is a pain in the ass, Sonia, so shut it. You'll be doing me a favour if you come."

"I wasn't going to look a gift horse in the mouth." She was laughing, "I was going to say that Geminis are schizophrenic."

We bought a newspaper and the raunchy *For Women* magazine on the way down the road.

"I think I've been unfairly treated all my life," she commented, flicking through the photographs of naked men.

Sonia and I had been going away together for the weekend since we were seventeen and stayed in her parents' caravan in Portrush. I was the fat friend, the silent henchman, who held her ice cream when she played *Space Invaders* and wolf whistled at boys. On one momentous occasion, the boy on the dodgem cars in the Amusements winked at me.

Things hadn't really changed, but fortunately the circumstances had matured. Now we brought a couple of bottles of wine with us and stayed in hotels. It was the only opportunity I got to feel glamorous. Jonathan and I were too busy saving to get married to go away together for the weekend.

Sonia was still the centre of attraction, even with cried-out eyes. We went to the gym and, after a quick surveillance of the weight-lifting machines, she selected the body with the biggest muscles and asked him to help her switch on the treadmill. Mr "I'm short so I lift weights" was only too happy to give her a guided tour of the gym equipment.

"You're never going to meet your handsome prince if you're not prepared to kiss a lot of frogs," she explained when I was teasing her in the hotel lobby after dinner.

Sonia had been running three miles a day for fifteen years. It was part of her hockey training when she played as wing for Ireland and, having been blessed with an addictive personality, she'd been hooked on the endorphin high ever since.

Personally, I was a bit suspicious of the "endorphin high" business. I went through a health and fitness phase for a brief period after I got engaged, stretching a bit and jogging to the end of the street and back again in the mornings before school. But then I met Mandy and Nicola Gorgon when I was red-faced and puffing, and the sound of their guttersnipe giggles still haunts my dreams. Maybe my endorphins died of embarrassment. The man from the gym waved from the bar.

"Don't wave back, Sonia," I pleaded, "or he'll come and join us and he'll probably have a fat friend with him, they always do."

Too late. Sonia waved energetically and he appeared beside her in a flash. Now he had his clothes on he looked quite cute, "Smurf" cute, like Jonathan. I didn't think him remotely attractive.

He bought us drinks, however, and said he wrote articles for *The Irish Times* and *Cosmo*.

"Oh," said Sonia, "so does my sister, Lynette."

"Lynette Anderson?" he said. "She has the nicest teeth and the sweetest smile." Before I knew it they were impressing each other.

I was used to being the fat friend in these situations. I picked up my paper and concentrated on the *Ballygowan Light* crossword.

My entire contribution to the evening's conversation consisted of, "What's the Irish word for 'donkey' please?"

They were talking about marriage. He was in full flow.

"Would you marry your best friend?" he asked. He said that most women (and he had a very low opinion of giggling women) say, "Oh, I couldn't" – but who the hell else were they going to marry?

"Do you think *Ballygowan Light* is low in calories or low in fizz?" I asked, rising to leave. I couldn't bear to hear the word "marriage". Everyone, Jonathan, Sonia, Smurf, they all seemed obsessed by it.

Sonia rallied well.

"Yes," she said with the stoicism and honesty of an alcoholic at an AA meeting, "it was quite obvious to everyone in the world that Paddy Butler should never have married me. Nine days out of ten he had no intention of marrying anyone. He would throw the word 'engagement ring' at me sometimes and even go on bended knee and propose to me, anything to stop me throwing things at him. And on the tenth day I caught him."

My mother has a theory about marriage as well. She says the spiritual state of "being married" rarely differs. She says everyone "is married" in the same way. So I might as well be married to Jonathan as to Paddy Butler or Smurf. It would all be the same at the end of the day.

"Well you were a bundle of fun, Marian," Sonia chided me when we got to our room.

"I don't always want to be friends with people who want to be friends with me," I said haughtily.

We met the Smurf again the following evening. We shared a taxi with him to the nightclub.

"Is your fat friend coming with us?" he asked Sonia.

"Marian isn't fat," laughed Sonia, "but she's got potential."

When we got to the nightclub he very chivalrously said, "If someone asks you to dance, Marian, don't feel you have to refuse them for Sonia's sake."

You could tell he didn't think I stood a chance. These townie boys are all the same. They lack imagination when it comes down to finding a woman "sexy". I think "thin and blonde" can get very tedious after a while.

So I left Sonia to him because:

a. She was thin and blonde

b. There were a pile of sixteen-year-olds mad to dance with me.

"Hi, are you married?" one asked.

"Hi, will you go with me?" said another.

"Hi, you're really sexy," a third informed me.

The only man in the place who I looked at twice was incredibly sexy in a strong tight way. He commented on my legs when he sat down beside me.

"She always sits provocatively," said Sonia who was

writing the DJ a note with her lipstick asking for more Lenny Kravitz, James Brown and Prince.

I wagged my finger at her. "If I was sitting with my legs wide open, that would be provocative," I said.

We got up to dance, my sexy tight man and me, and it was magic. He said he liked my freckled arms, but he didn't like my friend, she was a bitch.

"How much have you drunk?" I asked, but he grabbed my face and said "Stop talking, woman" and snogged me masterfully.

It was mega. Maybe the reason Jonathan was such a party pooper is because he didn't drink enough. Maybe he was repressed.

Maybe, I thought, I should be kinder to him. I must have been in a good mood.

When we got back to our seat Sonia and the Smurf were making sucking noises under his jacket to indicate a bit of nookie.

I yawned loudly. "Call me a taxi," I announced.

"Sure I'll leave you home," suggested my sexy bit. "My friend is sober."

I grinned. "Maybe I should find out your name first," I suggested. They were gentlemen. I told them I was a Protestant and Éamon said that he believed religion had been invented hundreds of years ago to help people live together, not to drive them apart. The driver offered me a cigarette and wanted to know what I was doing on Sunday night.

"I need a job," said Sonia on the way home. She'd slept till half ten. "My depression has more to do with having no job and no money than missing Paddy. I suppose it may also have something to do with not enough chemicals getting across my nerve endings. I think that if I had a glowing future ahead of me, a lot of my little problems would suddenly be very little. It's moping around indoors that's making me melancholy. And picking up boring men."

"Oh," I said innocently, "was the Smurf boring then, Sonia?"

Sonia laughed. "Careless talk costs lives," she said, "but Jimmy Fingers is a better kisser."

"You could go back to *The Rainbow's End*," I suggested. "You were always a natural at waitressing. Since it was bombed they've put a big extension on. I saw an advertisement for an assistant manager in the *Belfast Telegraph* last Friday night."

Just after my engagement, when I was enthusiastic about marrying Jonathan and blinded by the vision of two hundred guests, six bridesmaids, and a honeymoon in the Caribbean, I'd toyed with the idea of weekend work in *The Rainbow's End*, serving homemade vegetable soup, turkey and ham, and sherry trifle at wedding receptions. Sneaking home bits of wedding cake to practise with Jonathan. My mother told me it was a stupid idea.

"What do you earn in a weekend at *The Rainbow's End?*" she said.

I told her.

"Fetch me a pen and a piece of paper, Marian," she commanded, "and let's work this out academically. You can earn £15 a weekend, and the price per head of a turkey and ham wedding reception dinner at *The Rainbow's End* is?"

"£14.99, Mummy."

"Very well, for two hundred guests at £14.99 a head, Marian, you'll have to waitress at *The Rainbow's End* for two hundred weekends which is approximately four years, darling. So, in four years time, we can afford the two hundred guests. Now how much do you reckon a Caribbean honeymoon might cost?"

"Mummy," I protested, "it's the industrial self-sacrifice of young love," when she calculated that I'd have a bath chair and an ear-trumpet by the time the Caribbean honeymoon was paid off at £15 a week.

"I think," said my mother, "that some sacrifices are too much." Jonathan disapproved of the idea as well. He said we had our reputations to consider now that he was a trainee accountant and I was an English teacher. He said I would smell of fried chicken again. He said his friends were talking about him. Then *The Rainbow's End* was blown up so the decision was made for me.

"*The Rainbow's End,*" said Sonia, "I'm one step ahead of you, Marian, I had a job interview with Big Shirley on the Friday morning before we left for Donegal. It was a brainstorm that I suffered last week when I was lying in bed and feeling angst-ridden about my precarious future. I wore black velvet leggings to the interview because I reckoned that if I was any more glamorous I might have scared Big Shirley off. I wasn't a bit nervous. When the 2.15 pm interview time stretched to 2.30 pm, I was so cool I was going to chuck the application form into the bin. Did you know that they wanted my university qualifications? At *The Rainbow's End*? When you and I worked there people were being knifed outside the disco."

"Did you get the job?"

"Of course. I tell you Big Shirley was mad to have me back. I didn't have to remind her of how much experience I had. I told her I was footloose and fancy-free and the thought of pension plan employment made me want to gag. I sounded really glamorous and exciting, not like anybody's ex-wife."

chapter thirteen

We have an expression at home, "to calve a quilt with fringes." No one knows how it was derived, but once witnessed it isn't easily forgotten. Jonathan calved such a quilt when he realised I'd been stealing from the wedding account.

We had a row. It was utterly fascinating. We'd never really had a row before. I thought it was because we were too mature to shout and throw things but Sonia said it was because Jonathan always gave in. He was allergic to confrontation. In fact Jonathan was soft about everything except money.

"Don't be so selfish, Jonathan," I snapped. "Sonia's marriage has broken up and all you can nag about is a couple of hundred pounds."

"Sonia and Paddy Butler should never have married," said Jonathan pompously. "Everyone knew it would end in tears. If she had to be different, why didn't she marry a philandering Chinaman, or a philandering black man or a philandering man with one leg? No one would have minded, provided he was a Protestant. And they would have been a lot more sympathetic when it ended. If Sonia Anderson was my daughter, I'd have thrown her out of the house for marrying a Catholic."

For such a mild-mannered and uninspiring Smurf, Jonathan really was rather a bigot. It was Jonathan who told me, on our first date ten years ago, that you can tell Catholic and Protestant boys apart because Catholic boys always wear black training shoes. Nothing so poetic as their eyes being too close together. Like everything else he does in life, it's a slippy tit type of bigotry that slips out when his defences are down. Like someone trying to "talk posh", 99% of the time they get away with it. Jonathan, I suppose, is a book you shouldn't judge by its cover.

"Oh, really, Jonathan," I taunted, "and I thought religion had been invented hundreds of years ago to help people live together, not drive them apart."

Jonathan sniffed. "What concerns me," he said, "is that you insist on having six bridesmaids, two hundred guests and a honeymoon in the Caribbean, Marian. Sonia made her bed when she married Paddy Butler, let her go and lie on it now."

"Oh, time out, Jonathan," I pleaded. "I'm sorry for winding you up, I'm sorry I took the cash, I'm sorry I want six bridesmaids, two hundred guests and a honeymoon in the Caribbean. Sorry. Sorry. Sorry. Would it make it better if I kissed your feet?"

Jonathan looked sulky.

"Please don't sulk, Jonathan," I begged. "You know my

vestigial Christian Conscience won't let you go home still mad with me in case I die in the night, unforgiven."

Jonathan stood up. "Tell your mother 'thanks' for the tea and buns," he said. "You've really pushed me too far tonight, Marian. I'm going away for a fortnight to an accountancy seminar in Glasgow. I'll phone you when I get back."

And he stomped out without even kissing me.

Have a nice life, I thought. I locked myself in the bathroom and took off my engagement ring to give my hand a rest. My finger didn't look a bit bare without the solitaire . . .

"Marian," said my mother, "Marian, you left your engagement ring in the bathroom. You silly girl, you don't have to take a good ring like that off when you have a bath. It could get lost."

"It's insured, Mummy," I said.

"Even so, dear," she said, determined to have the last word, "Jonathan would never forgive you if you carelessly lost it. It means a lot to him."

More than it means to me? More than I mean to him?

On Saturday morning I visited Sonia as planned per Operation Entertain Sonia. She was playing her Blond on Blond album full blast and didn't look like she needed cheering up.

"God," she said, "I think I'm in love with Bob Dylan. I don't care what age he is, I would marry him tomorrow if he asked me . . . I've had my go at being a young man's slave, now I want to be an old man's darling."

"Why are you in such a good mood?" I asked sourly.

"Why have I never considered a career in hotel management before?" she countered. "I was a natural when I was at school."

She didn't need an answer. At the school we went to, if you were clever like Sonia, you did four science A levels and got a one-way ticket to university. If you were average, like me, you did arts and became a teacher. If you weren't clever enough for that, you weren't at our school.

"Now that I've grown up," said Sonia, "I want to be a function specialist. I want to spend every day for the rest of my life meeting happy adults and discussing weddings. I love talking about weddings because I've never had a proper one. Will you have a garter, Marian, when you marry Jonathan?"

"I shouldn't think so," I said.

"Oh but you have to have a garter so Jonathan can take it off with his teeth. And then he throws it behind him to all the bachelors at the party. And then you take a flower from your bouquet and throw it behind you and one of the spinsters catches it. And then the bachelor puts the garter on the spinster's leg."

"And the groom leaves wearing L-plates?"

Sonia laughed too. "Big Shirley has arranged for me to go back to college again and take a degree in hotel management. I went up today for the introductory session. It gave me a laugh. The lecturer was talking about being decisive in both management and personal life. He said he knew a man who had almost made it to the altar twice and backed out on both occasions. The thought of making a mistake terrified him. I nearly laughed out loud."

She grinned at me.

"Yesterday I thought about going to Dr Hennessey for tranquillisers. I haven't slept a wink these last couple of nights because, every time I shut my eyes, I have this horrible picture in my head of the day I left Paddy and him standing on the doorstep crying. It has been haunting me for days. I don't know why. We're broken up ages now and I'm not about to start feeling sorry for him. I cried too."

"Maybe a bit of grief therapy would do you no harm," I said gently. "People are getting face-lifts and therapists all the time in America. There's no stigma attached to it anymore."

"Well, I've changed my mind again," said Sonia. "I can't be melancholy when I've got responsibilities and can do no wrong career-wise. It's only a part-time course. I'll still be at home in the evenings to cook Bob dinner when he marries me."

Paddy Butler couldn't have timed his token-gesture reconciliation with his wife better. If he'd arrived on her doorstep a day too soon, she might still have been vulnerable enough to run back into his arms. And join the vicious love/hate/dependency circle where she'd left off. As for Paddy, I imagine he'd been through his nine other girlfriends and it was Sonia's turn again.

I arrived to take her shopping on Saturday morning, as planned per Operation Entertain Sonia. Mrs Anderson met me at the front door. She'd been on the gin and fags. I recognised the smell from when Neil died.

"I'm absolutely fucking furious with her," said Mrs Anderson, "I told her that she's making a tramp of herself with that husband of hers. Why can't she leave him with her head held high? Someday she'll leave him and have no home to come crawling back to."

"What?" I said, shocked. "Has she gone back to him?"

But Mrs Anderson was incoherent. "Oh, God," she said unsteadily, "the mistakes I've made with Sonia. I wish I could have had a daughter like you, Marian. You're so uncomplicated and so feminine and you always look so well. Like you exist in an ideal world, never worried, always contented."

Sometimes you'd think it was Mrs Anderson who'd married Paddy Butler and not Sonia. She'd neglected her in her formative years, both when Neil Mark One died and when Neil Mark Two was born (Neil Mark Two slept in his parents' bedroom till he was seven).

When I was fourteen I was trained to listen to my mother even if I didn't agree with her. Mrs Anderson is half a lifetime too late to assume the reins of command.

"Mrs Anderson," I said clearly, "please tell me what's happened and please stop crying, you'll make a frightful mess of your face."

Friday evening, the television blaring in the background and Sonia criticising her mother's cooking. "There are far too many complex carbohydrates in this meal, Mother." Paddy pulls up at 100 mph, beeps his horn. Sonia stops criticising mid-sentence, clutches her heart, goes white as a ghost, runs out of the back door in her sock soles, jumps into the car and it takes off at top speed round the bend in the road.

"And you're sure it was Paddy," I said.

"Of course it was Paddy," said Mrs Anderson maniacally. "Do you think my daughter could get another man to take her?"

"And you haven't heard from her since?" I said.

"Of course not!" Mrs Anderson shrieked. "I've never heard from her in twenty-eight years unless she wanted something."

"I think that's perhaps a little harsh, Mother." It was Sonia at the back door, still in her sock soles, looking sleepy, but her eyes were shining. Lynette's eyes used to shine like that when Jimmy Fingers held her hand. It's not difficult to recognise love when it slaps you in the face.

"So you're back," I said.

"I never went away," said Sonia defiantly. "Give me two minutes to change my underwear and brush my teeth, Marian, and I'll be down directly. Big Shirley says Bangor is the shopping centre of the universe so we'd best leave before the tour buses get there ahead of us and buy everything."

Mrs Anderson covered her face with her hands and wouldn't speak to either of us as we were leaving.

"My mother thinks romance is a game," said Sonia, "and it has only one set of rules and she makes the rules up as she goes along."

Shit, I was thinking, and she was doing so well. Almost normal again after a few Operation Entertain

Sonia outings until Factor X stuck his great big sexy head back into the equation.

"So," I said, "it was just a social call, was it? He was just passing the kitchen window at 100 mph and decided to say hello to his ex-wife."

Sonia started to laugh. "You are such a vicious cynic, Marian. I haven't seen him for forty days. Do you think I'm just going to run back into his arms when I've held out from crawling back to him for forty days?"

It was the language of an addict. "I've been without X for forty days and forty nights." For X insert your poison; chocolate, cigarettes, drink, Paddy Butler. How could it be healthy that, for forty days, every hour she'd thought of him, or tried not to think of him, or felt depressed when she wasn't thinking about him, knowing he was the cause?

It wasn't any of my business. She was my friend and it was my place to support her decisions, not make them for her.

"I was horrified when he drove up," she said proudly. "I didn't know whether to run towards him or away from him. So I ran towards him and I'm afraid it felt marvellous to put my arms around him again. I'd forgotten how he feels, what his skin is like, and his hands. Paddy always has warm hands. A pity his heart is so hollow."

Physically attracted and emotionally shipwrecked. There was probably a song about it somewhere. Something Jimmy Fingers would dedicate to Lynette if he was singing at a karaoke competition: *To the Girl Who Broke My Heart.*

I was becoming a vicious cynic like Sonia said.

"I'd rather you told me what actually happened," I said firmly. "Leave the *Mills and Boon* speculation to my furtive imagination."

"What happened is that Paddy dreamt I was giving birth to our baby or, as he charmingly phrased it, 'I claimed it was his'. And he was so excited at the thought of me bearing the fruit of his loins that he drove straight over after work and wanted me to start conceiving immediately."

"That's nice," I said, unconvinced. I know very little about love, but I know one thing. When you love someone your eternal optimism makes you a laughingstock. The words "It'll be different this time," are carved on your heart.

"Of course, if we got back together again, we would both have to be dead sure," she said bravely. "I couldn't live for another forty days without him again."

Brave words and no doubt she meant them, but I didn't know if she really believed them. All Sonia's life she had been clinging to a fantasy that one day she'd wake up and the luck in life that left her when Neil died would have returned in the night.

Lynette had a reading in Queen's University, Belfast that night. After our Operation Entertain Sonia trip to Bangor we were to pick her up at the train station, but Sonia decided at the last minute to get her hair permed in *Peter Mark*, so I collected Lynette alone.

"I'm only going to speak for fifteen minutes," Lynette

threatened when I met her. "They haven't mentioned payment and the first rule of self-employment is that, if you start doing work voluntarily, you are taken for a fool. Lynette Anderson Limited is not a charity."

Lynette once said something profound about her career-love situation when Jimmy Fingers jilted her. She said, "I don't care how successful I have the capacity to become. I will never again put my career ahead of my love life. A job can't love you back again."

I said, "Yes, Lynette, and if you only read for fifteen minutes, you'll be able to take the last train back to Dublin. But I'd stay here if I were you. My mother says 'Seldom Seen Often Admired'. It will do the boyfriend no harm to be without you for the evening. And, anyway, a little bird told me that Queen's Literary Society have bought in cases of free wine."

OK, I confess that it's blatant hypocrisy to be teetotal in Magherafelt and a drunkard elsewhere, but that's one of Life's Golden Rules. Don't shit on your own doorstep.

Jonathan has taken on two fanatically religious girls to help with the mortgage on the Belfast house. I think it's very insulting to assume that, just because there won't be sex in heaven, religious people are beyond criticism on earth as well. Jonathan lives with two girls and no one suspects him of three-in-the-bed orgies. That's another of the Golden Rules. If you say you're good-living, you get away with blue murder. We went to school with the tenants. Actually, Sonia used to speculate about their sexual preferences, because Tracy always wore her hair in curlers and thought she was a Barbie doll, and Sandra always had a page-boy haircut and never shaved her legs or under her arms.

We met Tracy on the stairs. She was all smiles and very sweet and wanted to make Lynette a cup of coffee. She made me nervous.

"I'm meeting Sonia at Rock Corner," I said quickly. "She said the perm would take two hours. She thinks Bob Dylan will like curly hair."

Rock Corner is where Paddy bought Sonia her engagement ring. It's the most exciting jewellery shop in Northern Ireland because half the window has new rings and half have been handed back.

There was an emerald, the spit of Sonia's, prominently displayed in the second-hand half.

I felt airsick, like I had a slow puncture. I didn't say anything to Sonia because I was too scared to. Sonia, who had been staring at it with her nose pressed to the window, didn't say anything either.

When we went back to Jonathan's house, Tracy made us all a nice cup of tea. Sandra arrived home from work in the middle of it.

"We went to school together," she said to Lynette.

"We did?" said Lynette.

Sandra Jackson has remained unmetamorphosed since the onset of puberty, but she was so physically forgettable she gave new meaning to the term "androgynous".

"You're looking different," said Sandra.

"Well I suppose you've never seen me in my pyjamas

before," said Lynette politely, "and I hope I'm better looking than I was at school. I got my ears pinned back when I was twenty. I'm glad people are still noticing. It was the first expensive thing I ever bought and I've been spending my money on plastic surgery ever since. I'm going for boob implants next year."

"I read your article about Bible censorship," said Sandra softly and I noticed Lynette stiffen. Fanatically religious people still scare Lynette, particularly the ones who say they've read her story in a knowing voice. Lynette changed religions after the Reverend Robinson affair. She goes to the Church of Ireland now. Because it isn't evangelical, she says. "Evangelicalism is arrogant, aggressive and non-human."

I hate the word evangelical, possibly because I don't know what it really means. It makes me think of the dreadful emotion-stirring missions the Girls' Brigade took us to as children, when I sat squirming in my seat waiting to hear God speak to me and propel me to the front of the church.

Lynette says the C of I sermons are always excellent, brief, well-delivered and relevant. Sometimes she gets lost in her prayer book, but she prefers the set prayers because she knows how long they'll last.

"And the church is painted yellow," she said, "nice and cheerful." Her greatest fear is that the charming Reverend will one day nab her on her way out the door and frogmarch her to the CAMEO (Come And Meet Each Other) tea and biscuits in the west wing.

"Well, of course I couldn't know somebody without reading their effort," said Sandra. "Have you written anything else?"

"Yes," said Lynette briskly, "I've just contributed to an anthology of Irish women's writing. I'll sign one for you, if you like."

Sandra smiled pityingly. "I never buy those type of books," she said. "You know I have an Honours degree in English, and I couldn't really comment on that type of book when I've read the best."

Professional to a T, Lynette was the picture of relaxation at the reading, in a brown wool sweater from *Kookai* and purple satin skirt from *Top Shop*. The fifth sentence of her piece had the word "erection" and, predictably, the undergraduates laughed. Lynette says she uses the word "erection" as an experiment with her audiences. If they laugh at "erection" she gives them the dirty readings. If they don't, she sticks to the clean stuff.

The private Lynette might have preferred to have been in Dublin with her boyfriend, sitting on his knee and gazing into his eyes, but you would never have suspected it. There was such a relaxed atmosphere in the hall I shouted, "What's nookie?" during the questions and answers.

Sonia sat beside me in a trance. If she didn't mention the ring she was going to burst and it was going to be very nasty. She disappeared after the reading.

"Where's my devoted sister?" asked Lynette. She'd been paid, she had a bottle of wine under each arm, she was prepared to smile. "Sisters," she sang, "there were never such devoted sisters."

I explained about Paddy's visit and the sighting of the ring. Lynette shrugged, uninterested.

"Everyone thinks their own tragedy is the worst ever invented," she said. "I had a pain in my chest for years after Jimmy Fingers jilted me. I was convinced my heart was broken and I have an A level in biology."

But I was worried about Sonia. Some people are born survivors, and some people aren't. It's just the way things are allocated.

"You don't think she'll do anything silly?" I said nervously. Lynette shrugged again. "Like put her head in the oven?" she said. "I hope not. I don't want to be the one who has to scrape her into a plastic bag and post her home." She smiled at my woebegone face.

"There's only one way to survive the pain, Marian, when the man you love doesn't want you, and that's to work until it comes out of your ears. Why do you think I'm so prolific? I sit down with a pen and a piece of paper and, hey presto, I'm away into a funny, light frothy world where even the rows are witty."

Sonia suddenly appeared at my elbow. "I've just thrown up," she announced, "and I feel much better."

"It might not have been your emerald, Sonia," I said.

"Well swept under the carpet, Marian," she said. "Of course it's my emerald. Didn't you notice the dent where I bounced it off his head the day I left? I don't know why I thought he'd keep it. I suppose I've been clinging to the romantic hope he'd put it on my finger again. Seeing it in the window of Rock Corner makes me brave enough to accept that he didn't mean it when he came back and said he thought we could still be happy. Now I believe things are over. There won't be a 'happy ever after'."

chapter fourteen

Sonia was lying in a convalescent heap in bed when she read that Vivien Leigh was a manic-depressive. This apparently was the reason she played Scarlett O'Hara with such power and conviction. She immediately gathered her depression into a neat little pile and decided to channel it into more creative endeavours than folding napkins at *The Rainbow's End*. She dragged me along to a reading of Magherafelt Drama Circle. Teaching has left me an unrepentant couch potato and I've absolutely no interest in middlebrow amateur dramatics, but it was better than being subjected, the Light Operatic Society, or Synchronised Swimming. Or sitting at home worrying because Jonathan had a mind of his own and was still sulking.

We knew nothing of the initiation rites of the Drama Circle so Sonia prepared a couple of audition pieces just in case they asked her. Shakespeare's "Let me not to the marriage of true minds" for the weepy or "The Owl and the Pussycat" to give them a laugh.

"So they can appreciate my versatility," she informed me. And indeed she landed the part of Heather the Whore (typecasting?). It was nothing to do with what I considered to be her acting ability, or the casting couch. Mr Stewart (in his role of producer, director, and principal boy) met us at the door of the school hall and said, "Which of you ladies is prepared to strip to your bra and knickers on stage and get into a clinch with me?" Star-struck Sonia elbowed me out of the way and said, "Me first."

I was flicking aimlessly through the magazine, the one with Vivien Leigh in it, trying not to watch the clock while Sonia practised stripping. I was bored. All the time, chronic boredom. Dissatisfaction with everything. With Jonathan, and with myself, and with the way my life was going. Would I feel any different once the wedding date was set?

Then my eye lighted on an advertisement for air stewardesses. I don't know why I read it and didn't just keep flicking. It was one thing I'd never thought of being. There's an impressionable age in childhood where every little girl dreams of being a hairdresser or an air stewardess and every little boy wants to play football for Manchester United. I was a victim of intellectual snobbery and a pushy mother. I was different even then. When tentatively, aged ten, I suggested that I might like to be a ballerina when I grew up, she quite ruthlessly nipped that ambition in the bud.

"Not after all the sacrifices your father and I have made for you, Marian," she said. "Over my dead body."

By "sacrifices" she meant elocution lessons, and piano

lessons, and swimming lessons and hockey sticks. "Sacrifices" were to be appreciated, not enjoyed.

So, had anyone bothered to ask, I would have pompously informed them that I wanted to be a barrister, or a nuclear physicist or a brain surgeon when I grew up.

It was the one torture that Stephen and I experienced together. Through my mother he had aspired to the ministry (of God, not the civil service).

So Stephen was also packed off to elocution lessons to improve his diction, and piano lessons so he could play hymns in Sunday school. Sacrifices were made for Stephen too, it's reassuring that he has turned out as wilfully ungrateful and useless as me.

I read the advertisement again. I seemed to fill all the categories. I could swim and speak English fluently, thanks to my mother's sacrifices. Weight had to be in proportion to height but, as applicants were only measured and weighed at the interview stage, I could start a starvation diet immediately. Twenty-eight was the cut-off age, and you had to be single. So, if I left it any longer, I wouldn't conform to the minimum standards. But I wasn't sure I could smile as convincingly as the girl in the photographs.

"I don't care," said Sonia sitting beside me. "If they were making *Gone With the Wind* nowadays it would be X-Rated."

Of course I consider myself frightfully puritan," I said, "but I imagine someone is bound to complain and Reverend Robinson will doubtless be paying another disciplinary visit to the Anderson house."

Sonia laughed. "I've nothing left to lose," she said, "We have already crossed swords the time he refused to marry me to Paddy Butler. Do you remember that? He said it was against the dictates of his conscience and would compromise his witness in the community. And of course there is no appeals tribunal with one's Christian Conscience, is there, Marian?"

Nicholas Stewart, the "most mature and interesting boy" in our class at school, was cast as Sonia the Whore's brother. Nicholas had got fat and tired-looking. He'd been going out with Stephanie Bruce for six and a half years and I imagined that took a lot out of a man. "Tower of Strength" Stephanie, he called her. They had no plans to get married.

"Jonathan and I have no plans to get married either," I said. Poor Nicholas, I thought, you were a handsome prince when we were at school, and look at you now. You've turned into a frog.

Sonia plonked herself between us.

"Nicholas is an old flame of mine," she announced loudly to no one in particular, "the first boyfriend I ever had with a car. The first night he phoned to ask me out, my father handed me a note that said 'type of car? colour? registration? age?' so that, in case he raped me, it would be easily identified. And I said, 'How am I supposed to meet boys, Daddy, if you think all my suitors are potential rapists? How did you meet Mummy?' He said he used to go and lig about the farmyard at my mother's place and the family got to know him that way. So I phoned Nick back and told him to bring warm clothes with him so he could lig about in our yard before he took me out, and we could all get to know him. Do you remember, Nick?"

She lit up a cigarette. Smoking was Sonia's latest favourite hobby. She believed a cigarette to be the ultimate creative accessory. When we were at school, she always carried sweat bands and shin pads and *Deep Heat* because they were hockey-playing accessories. Nicholas wouldn't take one of her cigarettes because a woman he sings with in his church choir was sitting next to us and he was afraid she might tell his mother he'd been smoking.

When I got home from the Drama Circle I locked myself in the bathroom, took off my engagement ring and composed a list. Air stewardess versus English teacher.

I didn't enjoy teaching. It was vocational employment and I hadn't been called. Sometimes I thought I didn't even like children. Not one pupil of mine had ever said she liked my engagement ring.

"Marian," my mother yelled in through the bathroom door, "you've been in the bathroom for half an hour. Jonathan is on the phone. Come out and talk to him this minute. You're a bit long in the tooth to be playing hard to get. What on earth are you doing in there?"

I was smiling when I opened the bathroom door.

"Planning my future, Mummy," I said. I put my diamond back on again before I spoke to him.

I'd tried talking to Jonathan about a career change once. He disapproved, naturally, and had invested an impressive amount of time and energy persuading me that I had a great job with great hours and the summer off.

"But, Jonathan," I'd said, "I'm not happy teaching."

"What has happiness got to do with it?" he'd replied. With that the subject closed.

"Hello, stranger," I said.

"Hello, Marian," he said.

Oh, well, I thought, it's going to be one of those conversations. Could he still be sulking about the theft from the wedding account?

"I haven't seen my fiancé for a fortnight," I said cheerfully, "and the best you can manage is, 'Hello Marian'."

"I've been having a good think this past fortnight," said Jonathan suddenly. "And I've decided to stop pussyfooting around the subject of our wedding, Marian. Indecision is a luxury, Marian, so I'm deciding for you. I've arranged an appointment with Sonia in her capacity of function specialist at *The Rainbow's End* for Saturday. And we're going to book the wedding. Perhaps we'll not get two hundred guests and six bridesmaids squashed into *The Rainbow's End* but, to be honest, I don't think we know two hundred people."

Usually I feel vaguely sorry for Jonathan because his only talent is his ability to blend, unnoticed, into the background. But I was impressed with this. Had he finally decided to sweep me off my feet?

"Can Sonia be one bridesmaid, then?" I said.

"You can have anybody you choose to be your bridesmaid," he said expansively. You could tell he was smiling.

"Yes, Jonathan," I said meekly. But it didn't sound like my voice saying it. Was I compromising, was he sweeping me off my feet? I got excited.

"What about Christmas, Jonathan?" I said. "I've always thought that was a nice time to get married. We could decorate everything with holly and ivy, save on the expense of fresh flowers and we could be videoed kissing under the mistletoe."

"Christmas?" asked Jonathan. "Do you mean in a month's time or next year? Don't be silly, Marian. Normal people don't get married at Christmas-time. I thought maybe Easter, myself."

I wasn't to be defeated. Not now I'd finally agreed to set a date. "Think about it, Jonathan, pet," I said persuasively. "People are organising and buying for Christmas for weeks in advance, and then you ask them, 'How was Christmas?' And everybody says, 'It was very quiet.' Our wedding could be the excuse for an enormous party."

"Of two hundred guests, perchance?" said Jonathan drily. "I think it's a mad idea, Marian. No one will buy us Christmas presents if they buy us wedding presents."

"For goodness sake, Jonathan," I said sharply, "how many pairs of knickers and socks does a man need?"

Jonathan ignored me. Jonathan had always treated lavatorial humour with the contempt it deserves. Sonia had tried for years to get him to laugh at a dirty joke.

"The appointment is for 2 pm, Marian. I shall collect you at 1.40. Try to be ready. It makes such a bad impression to arrive late, even it it's only Sonia we're going to see and she's never on time."

I couldn't sleep. There was a knot of panic in my abdomen and, when I closed my eyes, bright lights pricked at the lids.

Finally I sat up in bed and composed a vicious list of reasons why I didn't want to marry Jonathan.

It was the glasses which made him look like Toad of Toad Hall. It was the way his trouser legs flapped round his ankles at the end of his short legs. It was the way everything he did irritated me.

I wanted to make all the decisions in my life.

It was me who alternated between, "Let's leave the wedding for a couple of years so we can afford the six bridesmaids and the two hundred guests," and, "Let's go to the Caribbean and have no guests."

But I also wanted to be swept off my feet. Was that too much to ask?

When I still couldn't sleep, I composed a cover letter to the airline's London offices. I told them I was exactly what they were looking for in the line of air stewardesses. I was mature and sensible enough to encourage confidence in the most timid of fliers. I would enjoy the responsibility of putting passengers at their ease. You'd be surprised how an unassuming little frog like me could blow her own trumpet when she had to.

When I woke, I'd been invaded with a brash of pimples on my neck. And I'd ground my teeth so violently in the night my head was lifting.

"Look at me, Mother," I grumbled. "A tiny difference of opinion with Jonathan, it wasn't even a row, and look at the state of me."

My mother, with her unfortunate tendency to dish out advice with a trowel, repeated her life's motto, the Golden Rules she had drilled into me since childhood.

She said, "Happy marriages happen when the wife makes all the decisions, Marian, but she lets her husband think he has made them for her. When will you ever learn to sow the seed of what you want in his brain and wait till he works it out in his own time? I suppose you've been playing it all wrong with that boy again."

Ten years ago, as a hypersensitive neurotic adolescent, I would have burst into hysterical tears and immersed myself in Bible readings after such a scolding. Now I sometimes listened but, more often than not, I slipped tranquillisers into her tea. A few herbal stress tablets can make the world go round just that little bit more smoothly. Less rough edges after a herbal stress tablet, I always think.

"And Marian," she added, "go to the doctor and get that rash of pimples sorted out. That's what he's there for, after all."

I didn't like Dr Hennessey. He has attributed every problem I've ever had, from bad breath ("What have you been eating?") to woman's problems, to my weight.

"If you'd lose a stone, Miss French, you'd be a different woman."

He'd been telling me that since I was thirteen.

"Today it's my acne," I told him firmly. "No, I have not been bingeing on chocolates and greasy food, Dr Hennessey; yes, I wash my face every day, greasy hair does not hang in my eyes and I eat five pieces of fresh fruit and vegetables every day. I do everything that the textbook tells me to achieve blemish-free skin and I still have the ravished face of a fourteen-year-old. And I want it to stop now."

"Are you tense, Miss French?" he asked me kindly.

"No," I snapped. "What do I have to be tense about?"

Dr Hennessey smiled. "Acne on the neck is a hormonal problem," he explained. "It has nothing to do with the number of times you wash your face. Acne on the neck is caused by stress."

"So there's nothing you can do about it?" I asked, horrified. "Every time I have a row with my mother or my boyfriend I'm going to catch it. But, Dr Hennessey, that's not fair."

"I can give you some antibiotics to help fight off the inflammation." said the good doctor. "Are you on the pill? Because, if you are, these might affect its potency."

"Of course I'm not on the pill," I said, scandalised. "Keep your voice down, doctor, I'm not even married."

"The pill might help your hormones," said the doctor mildly.

On Saturday Jonathan and I inspected the new bomb-proof *Rainbow's End*. Mr Rainbow must have found a pot of gold among the rubble after the bomb. Everything was spanking new. But professionally I had a bad feeling about it. The Library had no books. The Banqueting Hall smelled of Conference Centre. The way Sonia bleated about the complimentary red carpet on arrival and the souvenir menus, you could be sure you were paying for everything else through the nose. Jonathan was magnificent the way he kept asking the price of everything, and Sonia was like a computer the way she could answer him. Jonathan said people thought you were stupid if you didn't keep asking the price of everything.

Eventually I sat down with a cup of tea and some game chips while Jonathan made one last check that the toilets flushed. "Come on, Marian," he said, "Drink up your tea and finish those crisps and we'll go. If you don't want them, bring them with you and I'll eat them in the car. Waste not, want not, Marian."

When we were in the car and out of earshot I said, "That Antrim Suite Sonia showed us will never hold

sixty people, Jonathan, no matter what Sonia says. It might hold forty if everyone breathes in. I was a waitress for years. I know these things."

"Too late," said Jonathan. "There was a cancellation on Easter Monday and I put a deposit on it, Marian. I paid for it with the Visa. Remind me to mark it down in the wedding account book when we get back."

My mother was delighted. Do you know what her secret fantasy has been all her life? She's dreamed of me getting married in her wedding dress on her silver wedding anniversary. It was such a simple thing to make her happy. Marry Jonathan and fade into comfortable obscurity. I think she would have forgiven me for being such a disappointment in every other field if I'd just done it.

So, to please her, I unearthed her wedding dress from

its box and began to fit it on. What a farce. I didn't even
fancy myself in it. I've seen bin-liner bags that did more
for a girl. I always dreamed of a hooped crinoline, a flash
of cleavage and a boned bodice, like brides in
photographs. That's why I'd been holding out for so long.
To be a fairytale princess on my wedding day. "It fits you
really well," my mother said encouragingly. "I think it's
predestination that you're a size fourteen too."

She was so delighted that the date was finally set she'd
have let me get married in a nightdress.

"I know it's a bit creased," she added, "but, if it's dry-
cleaned, that orange stain might come out. You're such a
lucky girl to have caught a man with respect for money,
Marian. When poverty walks in the door of a marriage,
love flies out the window." Once the dress was removed
and replaced in its box I sent my CV and the cover letter
on to the airline.

chapter fifteen

I had a terrible, restless night on Christmas Eve.

It was the horrible retarded adolescence of the Christmas Eve class reunion that did it to me. All year I dread it and its treadmill conversation. "And what are you doing with yourself, Marian?" Death-warmed-up small talk which invariably leads to cringe-making reminiscence. "I remember the time you said you couldn't wait to lose your virginity, Marian. You thought you'd have missed something if you died untouched."

But I'd kill myself if I couldn't forget. School was one of the most trying and desperate periods of my life but it was just like any other rut you might find yourself in. It was healthy to go to the reunion and remember that nothing stays the same forever.

Sonia refused to join in and play this year. She was having a Paddy Butler relapse and she wanted peace to do it privately.

"It's just because it's Christmas," she said. "It must be the saddest time of the year for a lot of people. Mummy used to dread Christmas after Neil died. There's such pressure on you to be happy."

"But sitting in front of the television every night is bound to make you depressed again. I'm sure if you got out and met people you'd feel a lot better."

"You're as bad as my mother," said Sonia. "She says I should get off my arse and find myself another man. As if anyone could ever compare to Paddy. Loving him has injured me for ever."

"Sonia," I said sounding like my mother, "lots of people suffer great disappointments. That's life. So there isn't much point in you crying your eyes out. If you were a writer like Lynette you'd consider yourself lucky to be given the opportunity to suffer. If Lynette was ever happy she would have nothing to write about."

"Well, I'm not brave enough to go through with the reunion," said Sonia. "I know my own limitations. I've been having nightmares at the thought of it all week. I can't decide which is worse, the ones who'll point and stare, or the ones who'll pretend to gush sympathy in the hope that I'll offer up the gory details."

"I think you're a mean spoilsport," I huffed. "You're the main course this year and you won't even humour us. If Lynette is prepared to sacrifice her dignity in the name of art, why can't you?"

Lynette never missed the Christmas reunions. She used them for research purposes, she said. And to test the "Jimmy Fingers" buzz factor.

"At the start I had jitters and nerves about seeing him from Hallowe'en," she said. "And it took to the following

Easter to recover my composure. I considered myself head over heels in love and well and truly devastated at that stage. Now it's just interesting to calculate how much my heart aches when I see him compared to last year. Whatever it's called, the thing that dances between us, it's a major source of inspiration in my life."

They met at the door of the rugby club. Lynette took a photograph of him in his Santa hat and he was inexplicably, gobsmacking rude to her and told her she couldn't get into the members' bar because it closed to non-members at 10 pm. (It was 10.02 pm). She would have to pay £3 and go upstairs alone to the empty, freezing, totally non-atmospheric disco. Yes, said Jimmy, Sonia was in the members' bar but no, she couldn't sign her in.

In the meantime Jonathan signed her in as a guest. Jimmy said, "You looked really fat on the *Kelly Show*, Lynette, immense even."

"Well, I've put weight on," said Lynette sweetly, "in all the right places. Sex and happiness does that to people, Jimmy. And you'd know anyway that the television puts ten pounds on you. My boyfriend and I stayed in the Stormont Hotel that night and our double bed was the biggest I'd ever seen in my life."

No surrender. Jimmy said, "Is that your natural colour of hair, Lynette?"

"No," said Lynette, "but you see these dark roots? That's the natural colour."

"I got my hair done in *Curl Up and Dye* for the *Kelly Show*," Lynette told me. "It sticks in my throat to say it but Mandy Gorgon is the only hairdresser in Magherafelt who has heard of setting one's hair in rollers. She was doing the routine chitchat about holidays till it was revealed that I was actually appearing with Gerry Kelly, not in the audience. She'd been wanting to know how to get tickets. Suddenly she couldn't fix my hair well enough. Nothing was too much bother, the last six rollers at the back of my head took half an hour to get right. People started to slip up the stairs to where I was sitting to get a better look at me. I was a celebrity by the time she was taking them out. One television appearance is worth a hundred newspaper features on the Magherafelt Roll of Fame."

Lynette was in a dangerous mood. She danced with everyone, laughed a lot and drank far too much and ignored Jimmy. In a perverted sense they were performing a unique, annual, animal courtship ritual for each other. Forward, backward, to, fro. If either of them stepped too close a firework exploded and they squared up for a fight.

Lynette is super-confident without being "super" if you know what I mean. I like it when she talks about places she's been to. From her I learned that Madeira was a great place to travel to if you're alone, and Ibiza town is full of homosexuals. These things would come in handy if I became an air stewardess. She was in Goa with her boyfriend just before Christmas. Goa really is the place to go(a). Posh papers talk about its geographical attractions, the tabloids tell you it's cheap. One of my favourite women's magazines did a feature in November about

166

perfume and described one of them as "a smell you expect on a beach in Goa".

"It was a bit primitive," she said cheerfully, "but I think the beds were bigger in India than here. We had a charming lizard in our bedroom which ate the mosquitoes. One sad little American man had his feet wrapped in bandages most of his holiday, suffering from mosquito bites. My boyfriend said, you can't go to a Third World country and expect British Standard BS5750 stamped on the weather and the wildlife."

She laughed. "World travellers that we are, there was one thing we couldn't have been prepared for," (glancing at Jimmy). "The second night we were there I dreamed I was being attacked by millions of mosquitoes who were eating the legs off me. Then there was a fearful banging and Jimmy broke the bedroom door down. It wasn't until breakfast that we discovered there'd been an earth tremor. The first since 1967, they said. It was the only time you made the earth move for me, Jimmy."

Lynette has an incredible talent for winding Jimmy up. He says she is the only person in the world who can make him lose his temper (and his head though he would die rather than admit it). "Of course, that's the great hang-up about being a professional writer," said Lynette. "You can never stop being 'aware'. Even on beach holiday."

"Pass me the sick bucket," said Jimmy.

He bought her a drink and she took Jonathan off to dance.

Patiently Jimmy sat down beside me.

Jimmy Fingers was behind the door when looks were being handed out. My mother, trying to be complimentary at a school speech day, once said, "He's very tall isn't he?" But he was born with a better talent than good looks. He could charm the knickers off you.

"Say, 'shit' again, Marian, I love the way you say it," he said. "I always looked forward to biology in school when I could sit behind you and Sonia and talk dirty. If a boy ever came near you, Marian, you ran a mile, and there were countless interested parties."

"But not yourself, Jimmy." I was lapping it up.

No, said Jimmy, he'd only ever wanted Lynette Anderson but she spent her life building barriers round herself.

"I always thought if those barriers were ever broken she'd be a wild child. Does she still write? I wouldn't say she does. It's not often you get her in such a good mood."

Then he went back downstairs with the male bonding rugby boys to play charades and the melodrama was over for another year. Donna Gorgon ("She's not my friend, she's my dentist") followed me to the loo. The fact that she'd made it as a dentist was very important to Donna. And who could blame her? It wasn't much fun being a "have not" at our middle class grammar school. Only by being a bitch from hell did she survive the big fish in the school pond. It must give the chip on her shoulder great satisfaction to be the big fish in the big pond now.

Donna calls her surgery "The Gentle Touch". I think that's hysterical because when we were at school she was the roughest heifer of us all on the hockey pitch. What she lacked in skill as a half back she substituted with brute force and ignorance. I still have scars where she lifted chunks out of me.

There was no modesty accompanying Donna's meteoric rise to dental stardom. "Came of nothing," said my mother, the honest oracle. "She doesn't know her place." On her surgery wall was every certificate she ever won. There was even one for under-fourteen hockey. The last time I visited she managed to inject me in the nerve. I bet she did it on purpose. I thought I'd been electrocuted.

While we were queuing for the loos I was subjected to the story of Lorraine Gorgon's life.

If you could believe all Donna said, Lorraine was a leading light in the psychological world. Donna said she got a letter last week. "Dear Dr Lorraine, You have been such an inspiration to women . . ." (Lorraine Gorgon? When had she been an inspiration to anyone?) Inviting her to a two-day psychological conference in Johannesburg in February. "I was a bit cynical," Donna roared (a habit she had picked up from shouting at patients over the noise of the drill). "It's my science background, Marian, I'm getting circulars inviting me places all the time. I told her she was on a mailing list and to ignore it. But not our Lorraine. She faxed them and told them she'd love to attend but couldn't afford it. And they faxed her straight back to her office in Queen's and offered to pay the whole thing for her."

Maybe I should offer myself as a specimen for one of Dr Lorraine's experimental studies. Somebody somewhere must want to study the life patterns of a marriage enigma like me. "The Female Afraid of Commitment." Libraries have been written about men who won't get married. They're analysed from their first nappy to their death-bed and all their flighty excuses recorded faithfully. A Paddy Butler case study is in there somewhere. But I've never heard of a similar study of the female of the species. In this role-reversal world, surely if men can be house husbands, women can fear commitment? When my parents got married their roles were clearly defined. Daddy put a ring on my mother's finger and said "My job is to put the meat on the table and your job is to cook it," and everybody was happy. I think things were simpler then.

I told Donna that Sonia and I had joined Magherafelt Drama Circle as I was washing my hands. I never bother washing my hands half the time after I've been to the loo, but Donna was watching and she's the sort of bitch who would talk about you. Cleanliness being next to godliness, Reverend Robinson might refuse to marry me if he suspected a trace of urine on my wedding finger.

"I studied drama when I was at Queen's," I said facetiously, "but Sonia is a natural. She's been offered a major part." No need to tell her my part was prompting behind the scenes.

"That Mr Stewart who runs it is nothing but a pervert," said Donna. "Mandy says he used to try and grab her breasts when she was going out with Nicholas at school. And the last time I was in the sauna he sat really close to me and tried to touch my leg with his."

Talk about giving a dog a bad name. I shrugged briskly. "You know, Donna," I said, "I'm beginning to feel discriminated against. I've never been sexually harassed in my life. What do you think I'm doing wrong? Sonia says it's because I don't smile enough. She's always being targeted too. The last time someone tried it on, she said, 'Take that chipolata away from me this minute, you silly little man,' really loudly."

Donna started to laugh. "Speaking of chipolatas," she said, diving into her handbag, "guess who this one belongs to?"

Sellotaped to the front of a Christmas card was a photograph of a naked Paddy Butler. My stomach heaved.

"That's tantamount to sexual harassment in its own little way, isn't it, Donna?" I said.

Donna started to laugh again. "Credit where credit's due, please, Marian. Paddy Butler and I may go back a long way, but I didn't pick myself out of the dirt to slide back into it again with him."

Back in the disco Jonathan was dancing with Stephanie Bruce. The tiny amount of human emotion and sympathy I possess I devote to Stephanie Bruce. What sort of a life has she had since Neil died? It's as easy and as common for someone to sink after a natural disaster as swim. Stephanie was a star at school, head girl, captain of the cross-country team, soprano in the school choir. She was a tower of strength type of person and we left her to sink. When Neil was killed we threw platitudes at her and comforted ourselves with them.

I remember saying, "He never knew what hit him, Stephanie, it would be worse if he'd lived to be a vegetable."

I remember Sonia saying, "He was going to finish with her anyway."

But we never wondered what she was feeling and we certainly never dreamt of asking her.

She bottled up her feelings, was the star at school and peaked too soon. She's the dental hygienist in *The Gentle Touch* surgery now. Tower of Strength Stephanie wouldn't have spat on Donna Gorgon if she'd been on fire at school.

Nicholas Stewart waved me over to the bar where he was chain-smoking with one hand and pouring tonic into his gin with the other.

"No spies around from your mother's choir, then?" I said but he wasn't in the mood for banal pleasantries.

"Marian," he said, "are you happy in your rut?"

"I'm not in a rut, Nicholas," I said stiffly.

"Yes, you are, Marian," he said, "you're in a comfortable rut and so am I. And I've decided that you can only be happy in a comfortable rut if you can't see how green the grass is on the other side."

So I had a terrible restless night on Christmas Eve. I dreamt that Jonathan ran away with Stephanie Bruce and everybody lived happily ever after.

My mother bought me a case of low-alcohol fizzy plonk as my Christmas present. My mother thinks it'll be just the ticket for the surprise engagement party she's planning for me but Jonathan and I know nothing about.

I met Lynette on the church steps after the carol service. "Isn't Reverend Robinson boring?" She yawned. "It's only because I'm the fallen woman of the congregation that I continue to attend when I'm home. Gives me a chance to dress up in all my swanky clothes and put my make-up on. So Mrs Mulholland and her cronies can see that I'm still at the 'pride' stage of my descent into hell and not the 'fall.' The old bitch said 'Merry Christmas, dear' to me and I almost trampled her. But I'm never going to drink gin again. I've never felt so depressed in my life."

"I'm going to Belfast," I said, "to find myself a wedding dress in the sales. It's either that or wear my mother's dress and it's horrible."

"No offence," said Lynette, laughing, "but no way am I coming with you to look at wedding dresses. I think weddings are contagious."

This year we had a wonderful Christmas dinner. So that bit wasn't an anticlimax, at least. I prepared the whole thing with unnatural diligence. We started with melon garnished with clementines and green grapes. Not particularly adventurous but Mummy chose it for sentimental reasons. She and Daddy had it at their wedding reception and, even if I couldn't get married on her silver wedding anniversary, maybe we could still eat what they ate. Jonathan and I had chilled cucumber soup and everyone else had the old faithful vegetable. The chilled cucumber was an experimental soup because I used to see, smell, touch and taste so much farmhouse vegetable, country vegetable, golden vegetable and plain vegetable soup when I worked at *The Rainbow's End*, that I still dream occasionally that I'm being chased by a bowl of it. I concocted a pilot run of chilled cucumber on Christmas Eve. Mummy took one mouthful and spit it out because she thought it tasted like hand-cream. Daddy dutifully spooned it into his mouth at lunch-time but said he had to wind down the car window and be sick on to Magherafelt main street on the way back to work. Actually, I wasn't so keen on it either after the first mouthful but Jonathan, as if to prove how much he loved me, ate a whole plate of it and asked for more.

Then we had Brussels pâté which mummy wouldn't eat because she wanted to know if they injected the Brussels sprouts into it.

Then we had salmon which was delicious and a real hit, then the turkey dinner (pause for digestion), then Christmas pudding and custard. The latter was a completely unnecessary indulgence. It's probably quite important here to note that at no time did I consider myself to be comfort-eating.

chapter sixteen

I was short-listed for the air stewardess interview in London to be held the very day of my mother's surprise engagement party for Jonathan and myself. Decisions, decisions . . .

So I cleverly swept the problem under the carpet and went wedding dress shopping with Sonia in Belfast.

Sonia was in flying form. "I've got bored being a sad, failed, disappointed woman," she informed me as she got into the car. "It's time I came out of my chrysalis and blossomed into the gay divorcee. So we're going to have make-up lessons in *Narcissus*, you and me. I phoned and booked them there before I came out. We'll be the best made-up bride and bridesmaid in the country after it."

"Don't frown like that, Marian," she added, laughing. "It's my wedding present to you."

"First," I said, "we're taking this fizzy plonk back to Marks and Spencer and swapping it for something drinkable. I can't hurt my mother's feelings by telling her I'd choke on a glass of fizzy plonk, but I'd be mortified to serve it up at an engagement party."

Sonia laughed. "Marian," she said, "you're an awful snob about wine for a teetotaller. How are you going to smuggle the bottles into your bedroom when you get back home?"

I could imagine it already. Everyone glued to The War of the Roses or Misery on the television, me sneaking outside to my car for the box of bottles and my mother appearing at the door. "What are those bottles, Marian? I thought I heard a clunking noise."

"I'd hide them at Jonathan's house if I was you," Sonia suggested. "Your mother has a nose on her like a sniffer dog. Remember the time you bought a packet of laxatives and they weren't in the house twenty-four hours before she found them and an inquisition was carried out. I always said you should have bought condoms, and edible underwear, and home pregnancy testing kits and dirty magazines, and blindfolds and stuff and left them lying round too, just to get her going."

I was violently intimidated in *Narcissus*. Not only were the make-up artists seven-stone Nicola Gorgon look-alikes but one received one's make-up lessons bang in the middle of the studio, with the hairdressing salon on one side and the waxing cubicles on the other.

"What brands would you usually wear?" my artist asked me.

I shrugged nonchalantly, thinking of the grubby sticks of reduced-to-clear items hiding at the bottom of my handbag.

"I'm very subtle," I said.

Beside me Sonia was busy telling her artist that Christmas Day had been the worst day in her entire life.

"My husband died, you know, before Christmas and not even trying really hard made it any easier. I can't always be brave, it's too tiring."

Well, of course, she had the entire attention of *Narcissus*. I would have sniggered at the audience except I was having my face thoroughly inspected and it was no laughing matter.

"I had six herbal stress tablets for my Christmas dinner," said Sonia, "and washed them down with the bottle of champagne we'd been saving for our first wedding anniversary. Just as well my best friend, Marian, arrived on the doorstep to save me . . ."

"The secret of successful make-up is all in the brushwork," my artist informed me. "The face is a canvas we paint on."

It took half an hour to paint in my acne scars and pat pancake studio make-up round my spots and make my face a "canvas". By the time she was finished Sonia had been made a cup of tea and given the phone number of Alcoholics Anonymous and I looked:

a. like I wasn't wearing foundation,

b. like I never had acne.

A prestigious social event. In silence Marian was marched to her pedestal. Harsh lines are passé this year. Eyeliner blended into the crease of the eye, lipliner covering half the mouth in feathery strokes . . . colours this year are vanilla, savanna and buff. An *au naturel* group of colours . . .

People started leaving Sonia and gathering round my pedestal and saying complimentary things about my face.

"Isn't it wonderful what a bit of make-up does to the plainest face."

I bought all the make-up and all the brushes and closed my eyes when I signed the wedding Visa (like crossing your fingers when you tell a fib, it doesn't make it as much of a sin).

"Can I have a pen and a piece of paper to make notes?" I asked. "Blending is a keyword, isn't it?"

Sonia was in a flamboyant mood when we reached the bridal department of Anderson and McAuley.

"Oh look, Marian," she screamed, producing a dress, "this one is gorgeous and it's reduced from £1,000 to £195. God, Marian, it's a Zandra Rhodes. Go on quick and try it on before somebody else sees it and snaps it up. It's brilliant for £195, isn't it? Not even your mother could be insulted if you bought your own wedding dress at that price. You'd still have enough left over for a three-piece suite and a set of matching cushion covers."

I didn't know if I liked the Zandra Rhodes dress or not. The bodice was white with unfortunate cheap-looking ruffles round the neck and arms and waist. The skirt was a peachy shade and there was no train. And the entire confection was synthetic polyester.

"But I don't like it, Sonia," I protested.

She sighed dramatically. "So, Marian, fashion guru *extraordinaire*, what do you like?"

"I want a hooped crinoline, a flash of cleavage, and a boned bodice," I explained. "I want to be a fairytale princess on my wedding day."

"This dress has a hooped crinoline, a flash of cleavage

and a boned bodice," said Sonia patiently, she was clutching Zandra very tightly. "If you don't want it, Marian, I'll buy it myself and save it till I've caught another husband. Now I'm a gay divorcee there'll be no stopping me."

So I fitted it on to please her. I'd never worn a bright colour or an eye-catching outfit in my life. Fat girls don't. We camouflage ourselves in navy blue. "Slimming and sensible," my mother describes my wardrobe.

Since we were fourteen it had been Sonia's mission in life to bully me out of navy blue. "Take it, Marian," she always said, "take it, take it."

She bought me a pair of multicoloured stripey leggings once and I wore them in bed.

I wasn't so fat any more, so maybe it was time for me to emerge from a chrysalis as well. I was taking my diet very seriously at last. There was method in my madness. It would be a bummer to be failed as an air stewardess for a few excess kilos. Alternatively, it's always said that a girl is at her lightest on her wedding day.

"Damn, damn, damn," said Sonia. "Zandra won't zip up the back, Marian. Either this dress was made for a midget, or you've put on a desperate load of weight over Christmas. You're going to be the fattest bride in the whole world at the rate you're going."

"Charming, Sonia," I said, huffed. "What size is it? Maybe there's a bigger, navy blue one on the rail."

She hadn't even noticed my weight loss. But then thin people don't. It's only fatties, who live to eat, who are neurotic about weight. My mother went through a phase of saying, "Hello, dear, you've lost a lot of weight," if she liked you and, "Hello, dear, you've gained a lot of weight" if she didn't.

It was my mother who started telling me ten years ago that inside every fat girl there's a thin girl trying to get out. So I didn't know why she wasn't more encouraging about my diet. She kept saying, "Why aren't you eating, Marian? I bet Neil Anderson wishes he could eat cheese sauce with his cauliflower today."

"Zandra is only a size ten, Marian," said Sonia. "I was starting to think it was from the children's department. You aren't pregnant or anything, are you?"

"Shh, Sonia," I said, mortified. "People will hear you. Of course I'm not pregnant. It's well seen you didn't attend pre-marriage classes with that dead husband of yours or you'd know that premarital sex is an abomination."

"Only if you get caught," said Sonia.

I didn't know why Jonathan and I didn't indulge in premarital sex. Even my mother said it was socially acceptable after couples got engaged. She gave me the phone number of a private doctor so I wouldn't have the embarrassment of begging contraceptives from Dr Hennessey.

I took my pill faithfully and well. It was summertime and my skin cleared up and I had a tan from the week in Cyprus.

I was prepared to respect him in the morning.

"I've got subtle lighting," I confided in Sonia, "and the sexy music and the flattering underwear. Do you think I need anything else?"

"Is the underwear navy blue?" said Sonia.

We had a bottle of champagne, and I undressed in front of him in the bedroom. It was a hot night and he was wearing only boxer shorts in bed. I got in beside him and waited for something to happen. Finally he rolled over and kissed me on the forehead. "When you play with fire, Marian," he said, "you have to expect to get burnt."

I stopped taking the pill. It was making me fat.

"What you don't have you don't miss," I told Sonia when she suggested that Jonathan must be religious or impotent or gay. Getting pregnant out of the sanctity of marriage was the most dreadful nightmare of my life, actually, or the most desperate fantasy, whichever way you want to look at it.

I had a fantasy where Jonathan and I went to Reverend Robinson requesting to be married and he asked, "Is there any reason why you have to get married?" looking pointedly at my belly.

"Oh yes," I said happily. "We're having a baby."

"And are you happy about this, Marian?"

"Oh yes, Reverend Robinson, we love each other."

And Reverend Robinson refusing to marry me because marrying a girl who wasn't ashamed of being pregnant outside wedlock was against the dictates of his conscience and would compromise his witness in the community.

And Jonathan and I trekking barefoot, knocking at doors and taking out advertisements in the paper, begging for another minister whose conscience dictated differently to Reverend Robinson's to marry us.

"When you play with fire," I told myself occasionally, "you have to expect to get burnt."

We put Zandra Rhodes back. The price was tempting. I could imagine my mother saying "A designer dress? Why didn't you snap it up? You could have had a couple of ribs removed for your wedding day."

But one hooped crinoline, flash of cleavage and boned bodice looks very much like another when you have an enormous question-mark hanging over your head. The air stewardess interview or the engagement party? I needed another carpet to sweep it under.

"Let's stay in Jonathan's house tonight," I suggested, "and drink some wine and go out for a Chinese. My weight hardly matters when I can't find a frock to fit me."

We drank four bottles of wine between us before we went to the Chinese. After the second bottle my neck went a horrid blotchy pink.

"You better buy a wedding dress with a collar," Sonia advised. But after the third bottle the blotchiness went away.

"Did you know," said Sonia as we stumbled into the Chinese, "that those who drink a bottle of wine a day are medically considered to be alcoholics?"

"Let's have some Chinese tea to start," I said unsteadily, "and would you give me a cigarette to focus my attention so I don't throw up. I think I've had one bottle too many this evening."

"Charming," said Sonia, "I don't feel so hot myself, actually. That cigarette will only make you feel sicker, Marian."

The advice came a fraction too late. I took an inexperienced drag and made a violent lurching dash to the Ladies.

Oh God, I thought, four bottles of wine was well over the medical alcoholism limit. If I choked on my vomit and died, I wouldn't have to decide whether I wanted to be an air stewardess or Mrs Lamb. It would be the ultimate act of sweeping things under the carpet.

I lay down on the tiled floor and thought about being dead. An American woman stepped over me and said, "I know just what you're feeling, honey, I was an alcoholic for fifteen years." If I was dead, I thought, it wouldn't be my problem. Then I stuck my fingers down my throat, threw up on the tiled floor and felt much better. Perhaps there would be no need for cardiac massage, artificial respiration and an embarrassed funeral after all.

Sonia was forking prawns and cashew nuts into her mouth when I stumbled back.

"Sorry to be a party-pooper, Sonia," I whispered sitting down, "but I've just thrown up on the floor of the Ladies and now I'm going to run away and leave it for somebody else to clean up."

Sonia began to shovel my beef and oyster sauce into her mouth. "It's not like you to be like this, Marian," she said. "Have you something on your mind?"

I signed the wedding account Visa for a quick getaway, and fell over the front step on the way out.

In the midst of my morning-after hangover, I made a decision of sorts. I would persuade my mother to change the date of the surprise engagement party to Valentine's night.

And to soften the blow I'd offer to wear her wedding dress. Hooped crinolines and a flash of cleavage and boned bodices would have to wait for another day.

I used to say, "Do you want the good news or the bad news first?" when I wanted something from my mother but she always wanted the bad news and that spoiled the rest. So in one breath I said, "I'd love to wear your wedding dress, Mummy, when Jonathan and I get married, but could we change the date of the surprise engagement party to Valentine's Night? Aunt Angela has invited me to London to help me choose my going-away outfit."

"What a good idea," said my mother cheerfully. "Your Aunt Angela might never have managed to catch a husband but she has great taste in clothes."

Then I asked Jonathan to come to London with me. It was a test, I suppose. If he came with me, we'd choose my going-away outfit together, if he didn't I'd go to the air stewardess interview.

In my own way I was as pathetic as Sonia the day she made a pact with God before her maths A level first paper. Sonia thought that, if she heard *Kayleigh* by Marillion on the radio before she went into the exam, she'd get an A in the exam. She should have listened to that Garth Brooks song about some of God's greatest gifts being unanswered prayers, instead.

"Jonathan," I said seductively, "I saw the loveliest Byzantine wedding rings in the bridal magazine this month."

"You wasted money on a bridal magazine?" said Jonathan. I sighed. "No Jonathan," I said patiently, "I looked at the pictures in the shop. Why don't you come with me to London and we could choose one together in Michael Rose's Ring Room in the Burlington Arcade? And you could help me choose my going-away outfit instead of Aunt Angela."

"Don't be so stupid, Marian," said Jonathan. "We can't afford to be jetting off to London at the drop of a hat. I'm not a rich man, Marian."

"It's just as well I love you then," I said ominously, "for everyone knows that you should only marry once for love and the rest of the time for money."

"We'll be able to afford weekends in London after the wedding," said Jonathan gently. "At the minute, pet, we have to concentrate on saving to get married. It's not much longer now."

"Jonathan," I wanted to shout, "forget about saving to get married. I've got an air stewardess interview in London. Just for once in your well-structured, well-scheduled, well-accounted-for life throw caution to the winds and sweep me off my feet."

I said nothing and he kissed me on the forehead and went home. My mother said, "Not that I was listening or anything, Marian, but I think you give Jonathan a hard time. You're a very lucky girl to be marrying a man with respect for money. When poverty flies in the door of a marriage, love flies out the window."

I went to bed in a huff. Sometimes I pitied my mother, thinking her a victim of her own respectability. And sometimes I thought she didn't know her arse from a hole in the ground.

She came slipping into my bedroom about midnight.

"I'm sorry I shouted at you, Marian," she said. "I felt bad about it afterwards."

Then she said, "Marian, do you really think you're going to be walking down the street some day and suddenly fall madly in love with someone else for the rest of your life?"

Perhaps, I thought, and when I do I'll wear the hooped crinoline, with the flash of cleavage and the boned bodice.

chapter seventeen

My mother, in her wisdom, decreed that I take the big
suitcase to London for my two day interview/visit to
Aunt Angela. I was dispatched to the attic to find it and,
while I was gone, Stephen lifted my hairdryer out of the
small bag and hid it. Stephen has found himself a
girlfriend and with one leap has left his adolescent rut
forever. We have mouthwash and various foul-smelling
aftershaves in the bathroom now and he uses the diffuser
on my hairdryer to calm his frizzy hair. My mother still
hasn't been introduced to her. It went to prove he was a
late developer all along.

I freaked when I realised he'd hidden the hairdryer.
It's a bit embarrassing for a girl who wants to be an air
stewardess that I was so excited about taking the shuttle
to London. Excited, aflame, agitated, aroused, awakened.
There's a whole thesaurus of words to describe what I was
feeling. I was also nervous, overwrought, and very
seriously hot and bothered.

"Are you stealing my hairdryer, Stephen?" I screamed, "give it back or I throttle you with the flex, you pansy."

Of course my mother pounced on me. We haven't had a decent screaming match in weeks but, if Stephen knifed me in cold blood, I think she'd think of an excuse for him doing it.

"Your face is all clapped in, Marian," she said severely. "That's how *anorexia nervosa* starts. Fat girls get excited when a diet finally works for them."

But really she was only concerned that her wedding dress would be too big on me.

I had rather cleverly included my mother in all the wedding arrangements. Including her for the same reasons that people invite their next-door neighbours to a wild party. People, especially parents, hate to feel excluded. "A girl should look her best on her wedding day, Mummy," I said. "And no one should outshine the mother of the bride." And we've been grooming each other like chimpanzees in love ever since.

I took her to a really posh hairdressers in Belfast for her birthday present. A man Aunt Angela used when she read the news from the Belfast studio. A man who understood middle-aged hair, and middle-aged ladies.

"I hope he'll be a bit effeminate," she said, "so he won't intimidate me."

In fact she liked him so much she was loudly lamenting the fact that Stephen hadn't become a hairdresser as we were leaving.

I had a facial in *Narcissus* while I was waiting. No point in having the make-up and the notes on how to apply it, if my face resembled cottage cheese instead of canvas.

"But they're only little spots on your face," said the beauty therapist. "I don't know why you're so worked up about them."

"I don't see any spots on your face," I said bitterly.

"That's because I squeeze them," she said. "Forget all that stuff about letting nature take its course, that's for girls with beautiful skin. The minute you see a spot, squeeze it. "

I lay down on the slab, the sacrificial lamb, while she examined my face under a light.

"It's not often I get such a dirty face," she said cheerfully. "Such a challenge."

I felt butterflies in my stomach like I used to feel on the approach of the Gorgons at school.

"I have a very low pain threshold," I whimpered, wimp-like.

"A facial is useless without extraction," she said severely, waving a freshly dislocated blackhead under my nose. "This is the biggest blackhead I've ever seen, you could win prizes with blackheads like these."

I closed my eyes to stop tears bouncing out, ground my teeth, suffered to be beautiful. I was never going to bed again without taking every scrap of make-up off.

Finally it was over.

"I'll expect to see you in a month's time," she said, "the more facials you have, the softer the skin gets and then we can really get at the stubborn blackheads."

I smiled bravely. "Or I could just take a Brillo pad to my face," I said, "it wouldn't hurt as much."

One of the Nicola Gorgon look-alike make-up artists recognised me.

"You're Marian," she said, "the angel of salvation. The best friend who saved Sonia's life on Christmas Day."

I made a run for it.

"Your hair's a bit frizzy at the back," my mother commented critically as we hoisted her suitcase into the car.

I shrugged. "I'll bring the gas curling brush to the airport with me," I said, "and smooth it out on the way."

"Mummy," I added, "I'm not convinced that blue eyeliner suits you."

"Let Angela help you choose a going-away outfit," she shouted after me as I went through Departures. "Or better still borrow one from her."

My mother's suitcase got chewed up on the baggage carousel in Heathrow and a large hole ripped in the side of it. The suitcase contained all of my new life, the face products and my manual of good grooming. Everything, in fact, except my toothbrush and a pot of Vaseline. Vaseline is my desert island discs luxury, to lubricate my lips, soften my eyebrows for plucking, and to rub in my nails night and morning so they don't flake.

In a dream me and the insurance man stuck it together again and I put in an insurance claim. He was a nice man and he said I'd probably get a new suitcase, which would please my mother at any rate.

I nipped into the loo to powder my nose and comb my hair again before taking the tube to Angela's house.

Angela laughed when she saw the ripped suitcase.

"I'm not sure you've got the temperament to be an air stewardess," she said. "Remember the time you were at school and missed your flight to France because you read the ticket wrong? And now your baggage is in pieces. Bit of a dodgy track record for air travel, isn't it, Marian?"

I'd told Angela all about my air stewardess interview in the hope that she'd give me some free cosmopolitan advice. "I need to look like I've had a lifetime of good grooming," I explained. "All the air stewardesses on the shuttle had nail polish that matched their lipstick and lipstick which matched their uniform. I can't even decide what shape of wedding dress suits me."

"As good a reason as any for not getting married," said Angela drily.

"You don't have to approve of me bolting on Jonathan," I said quietly, "but do you know what the alternative is, Angela? We were at a pre-marriage class last night and Reverend Robinson said that according to the Bible there had to be one captain in a marriage and the captain had to be the husband."

Angela shrugged. "I grew up in Magherafelt too," she said, "and the minister used to preach sermons about university exerting an evil influence on young people and how the heart can harden to God rather like plasticine which has been left out of an airtight box. And then he had the face on him to shake my hand after the service and say how wonderful it was to see me out. I was always as much of a hypocrite as him. I always shook his hand and never punched him on the mouth."

Silly me. I ate a chilli, crunch, crunch, at dinner thinking it was a green pepper and it almost blew the head off me. I'm quite sure the chilli was the reason I woke at 2 am with violent stomach cramps.

It was a blessing in disguise. I was at my lightest for years at the air stewardess interview.

Was I a success? Who knows. My nail varnish matched my lipstick which matched my interview suit, thanks to Angela.

And the questions. I've never managed to crack "occupational psychologist" questions and I couldn't ask the careers officer at school for advice because then everyone would know I was looking for another job. Lovely Lorraine Gorgon probably instigated such stinkers as "Where do you see yourself in five years' time?"

I saw myself married with a couple of neat children. I did not see myself footloose and fancy-free which, let's face it, at thirty-three was the brave face of desperation. My strengths and weaknesses?

"Quite often they're the same, aren't they?" Angela had suggested at my briefing. "For example, assertiveness is good on some occasions and not so good on others."

"Have you travelled much?" they asked.

I began to sweat in my interview suit/going-away

outfit. Soon my face would be as crimson as my jacket. Angela had suggested crimson. She said crimson lipstick would brighten up my "interesting" face. She advised me to make a bonfire and burn all my sensible navy blue.

"Oh yes," I fibbed cheerfully. French conversation holidays as a schoolgirl and two package tours to Cyprus could hardly be described as "travelling". "I was in Goa at Christmas." Lynette had shown me her photographs of Goa. There had been a lot of sand and not much action, she'd said.

"It was lovely," I said knowledgeably, though I would have failed any English student of mine who described a country as "lovely". "Third World countries often are if you don't expect British standards."

"Are there a lot of gays in Goa?" he asked.

Gays? Did he mean homosexuals or jolly people? I couldn't remember Lynette mentioning the word gay. Hippie, yes, but gay?

He thought it was peculiar that I'd travelled alone, had I no friends?

By the time I was leaving, sweat was dripping from my forehead and I was convinced they thought I was a lesbian nymphomaniac who toured the world in search of the ultimate gang-bang. Little did they know I'd postponed my engagement party to be there.

That's it, I thought, I've fluffed my only chance of escape. In a tearful haze I took the tube to Piccadilly and walked to Burlington Arcade and Michael Rose's Ring Room.

My crimson lipstick was smeared halfway across my

face, my mascara was trickling down my cheeks and my nose was bright red from pressing it to the glass of Michael Rose's Ring Room.

"If he bought me a Byzantine wedding ring I'd marry him," I said loudly and a little old lady who'd been passing stopped and looked at me.

"He says we can't afford to buy a bridal magazine, let alone a Byzantine wedding ring," I said. "All he thinks about is the price of living happily ever after."

She handed me her handkerchief silently.

"When I die," I said, "the words 'Saving to get married' will be engraved on my heart."

When I got back to Angela she said, "Oh dear, maybe we should have invested in waterproof mascara."

She had two presents for me. One for each decision. My engagement present was a Pre-Raphaelite picture of a Greek girl dreaming beside a pool because, Angela said, if I married Jonathan I'd spend the rest of my life on package tours in Greece dreaming about what might have been, not that she was trying to influence me in any way.

I started to cry again. "My interview was a disaster," I said dramatically, "so I'm not even going to get the chance to decide if I want to bolt on him or marry him after all."

My other present, my world-travelling bolter present, was the most wonderful green tin hippie suitcase with purple flowers painted on it.

"I bought it in Goa," said Angela, laughing. "I went on a package tour a couple of years ago."

"And I suppose it was lovely," I said bitterly.

"Not quite the adjective I'd use," said Angela. "However, the native I bought the suitcase off told me it was very good quality. So, either I have an unsurpassed eye for quality, or shop owners can see me coming a mile off. Now you're in league to be searched for drugs by customs from here to Timbuktu. I mean, who but a drug-carrying hippie would carry such a suitcase?"

"The girl looks like her boyfriend bullies her about the price of everything," I said, admiring the Pre-Raphaelite picture. Then I said, "Do you know what I really want, Angela? I want Jonathan to arrive on a black horse, or in a black car if we're being prosaic, and say, "I won't let you bolt and become an air stewardess, Marian, you aren't getting away from me. You're going to marry me and I'm never going to let you out of my sight again."

"And you would drive off together into the sunset and live happily ever after?"

"Now you're laughing at me," I said. "You think I'm grasping at straws. If he really loved me, why wouldn't he climb mountains and swim rivers to make me happy?"

"Life isn't a fairytale," said Angela. "Men aren't handsome princes who work nine to five slaying dragons and rescuing damsels. And women aren't just pretty faces they come home to. Sometimes men need to be ridden up to and rescued the same way as women do."

Jonathan wasn't at the airport when I flew home. Call me old-fashioned, but I had rather hoped for a welcoming committee. I lifted my tin suitcase off the carousel (everyone smiled kindly) and had paraded a couple of times up and down in front of the terminal building before he pulled up.

I wanted to smile and kiss him but I felt cross. Then I felt guilty about the way my irritation had spoiled a potentially wonderful reunion.

chapter eighteen

Hubble bubble, toil and trouble. Another showdown for
Jonathan and me? The Drama Circle's dress rehearsal was
on Valentine's Night. I had a tension headache all day
worrying about how I could break it painlessly to
Jonathan. Nicola Gorgon yawned once too often in
English and I tore strips off her.

I don't have to emphasise that Jonathan considered
this to be the straw which broke the camel's back. First
he told me I was being stupid.

"You're being stupid, Marian," he said, "Of course
we're going to have our engagement party on Valentine's
Night. You can give the Drama Circle a miss for once.
You're only the prompt after all, hardly the star."

"'Continuity'. I'm called the 'continuity person'."

There was a noise on the other end of the telephone,
as if Jonathan was banging his head against a brick wall.
"You could start the party without me," I suggested, "and
I'll come along later."

"You want to come late to your own engagement

party?" asked Jonathan. "The party will be worthless unless you're there. How can I announce our wedding date if you aren't there to announce it with me?"

"You could use a stand-in," I said, "then I wouldn't have to come at all. I'm sure Stephanie Bruce could do a 'Marian French' impersonation for the evening."

"Stephanie Bruce?" said Jonathan. He was gnashing his teeth. "Over my dead body."

"Well, then," I said, "the alternative is that we have the party on the night after Valentine's Night. You could make sandwiches and buns for it on Valentine's Night while I'm at the rehearsal."

"Make buns," Jonathan repeated, parrot-like, "you've got to be joking, Marian." And he put the phone down on me. I made a decision, if I got the airline job I wasn't going to marry Jonathan. Over my dead body.

My mother watched me wipe away a few sad little tears of self-pity.

"It's all your fault as usual, Marian," she comforted. "Chopping and changing the date of the party without taking other people's feelings into consideration."

"You're still wearing that blue eyeliner," I said, "and it still doesn't suit you."

My mother shrugged. She still insisted on having the last word in everything. "At least I'll get a card on Valentine's day."

I was scoring red pen through Nicola Gorgon's essay "Why School is a Waste of Time" when Jonathan phoned back.

Oh, shit, I thought uncomfortably, not another "much ado about nothing" row. I'll never get this marking done.

But Jonathan said, "We're both too old for stupid games, aren't we, Marian? I've got the cookery book here in front of me, opened at the 'Bun' section. Will I start with 'A' for Afghans and Almond Bars and just keep going till I get to the Yo-Yo Biscuits?"

"Oh, Jonathan," I said impulsively, "I do love you," and I was almost sure I meant it.

"And I love you back again," he said, "so I'll be putting my foot down about our wedding after the play and not before. For some reason, I think that would achieve nothing."

He even sent me roses on Valentine's Day, something he hadn't done in years.

At the dress rehearsal Sonia sat down beside me and said, "I like that crimson lipstick, Marian. Do you know how I was in love with Paddy for twenty-four hours a day, seven days a week for fourteen years?"

"Not that old sausage again, Sonia," I protested.

"Yes," said Sonia, "that old sausage again, and you remember how I made that speech at my wedding about opposites not attracting and how I loved Paddy because I saw myself in him."

"I might," I said.

"And you know how your mother advises that you marry for love only once and the rest of the time for money?"

Something started to twig in my head. It was in the final scene of *The Chastitute* when all the cast were draped orgy-like over each other on stage and Mr Stewart was making his final tragic monologue with a shotgun in one hand and a whiskey glass in the other and every time he said something heart-rending, the cast laughed demoniacally at him.

Sonia and Jimmy Fingers had been draped over each other since the start of the rehearsals and Sonia always complained about the way Jimmy stroked her "shampoo and set". At the last rehearsal, Nicholas Stewart had swapped with Jimmy and I noticed him kissing the inside of Sonia's arm enthusiastically.

She was smiling like the cat who got the cream.

I glanced over to Nicholas who was chain-smoking in a corner. Stephanie was with him. At the rehearsal with him on Valentine's Night I noticed that she kept trying to hold his hand and stroke his leg and he looked like he was going to freak.

"Nicholas isn't married to her," said Sonia, following my gaze, "he doesn't belong to her."

"You Andersons have a wonderful talent," I said drily. "You've single-minded, tunnel vision ambition. I'm madly envious of your tunnel vision ambition. Look how Lynette went single-mindedly and became a great journalist."

"Wee puke," said Sonia sullenly. I don't know if she meant Stephanie, or Lynette, or me. "One passionate love/hate relationship is enough in any lifetime. And Nicholas has a handful of hairs on his chest, just enough to prove that he's male. And anyway," she added as an afterthought, "I don't know what he sees in Stephanie

Bruce. You could pack luggage into the bags under her eyes."

"I'm having nothing to do with it," I said primly, "I have troubles enough of my own." Turning into my mother again.

During the interval, when I was drinking tea and sharing half a *Hob Nob* biscuit with Stephanie ("Please eat the other half, Stephanie. Now I've gone anorexic, a whole biscuit would kill me"), Sonia ambushed Nicholas Stewart behind the scenery.

"You did what?" I said, shocked, afterwards.

"I thought you didn't want to know," said Sonia gleefully. She shrugged. "How did Mandy Gorgon get so many boyfriends when we were at school? It doesn't take an A level in biology to know a man can't resist a woman who blatantly desires him. It's a genetic weakness in them. Paddy always used it as an excuse when he was rambling. 'She threw herself at me, Sonia, it's a genetic weakness playing up.'"

To be honest I sniffed a bit. For one, I was jealous. The first really reputation-ruining incident in Sonia's life was the time she thought she was pregnant because Nicholas kissed the back of her neck in the caravan in Portrush. And avoided her like the plague afterwards. The caravan affair had soothed my inferior soul because it proved that Sonia Star could bend and break like the rest of us. She couldn't get what she wanted all the time. Now it seemed, metaphorically speaking, that she was right back where she started at fifteen. Only this time it was going to be a success.

After Neil died, Sonia used to have a daydream fantasy thing about his ghost. Initially the ghost followed her round and sat beside her at school and chatted to her when she was alone, studying, or running, or in bed trying to sleep. She was so convinced it was there, and so convincing, that one time when I slept over at her house after a stint in *The Rainbow's End*, I woke at three trembling uncontrollably. I had to get out of bed and walk around to stop shaking. I was sure the ghost was in the room. As time went on, and the shock of the death lessened, the ghost stopped talking to Sonia, and stopped visiting her room and she could only see it beside the grave. Now she only visits the grave at Christmas and she doesn't see it any more.

As if she was reading my mind, Sonia said, "Paddy and I were only destined to have a love affair, weren't we? The night before we got married we went for a late drink in *Grubb's Pub* and when we were knocking the back door to get in after closing, I remember saying, 'I can't believe we're getting married in the morning.' And he laughed and said, 'I can't believe it either.' Nicholas and I go back a very long way, Marian, right back to the very start. I'm not going to mess it up this time."

I still sniffed.

Prude that I was, I didn't believe that all was fair in love and war. Stephanie Bruce was chasing the same nightmares as Sonia.

But Sonia said that a relationship is not an endurance test. You don't get service medals in love.

chapter nineteen

It was the première of Magherafelt Drama Circle's production of *The Chastitute*. Mr Stewart gave us a pre-play pep talk (PPPT) and reminded us that, since Magherafelt qualified as Presbyterian suburbia, it was the closest a lot of us would get to heaven and we were not to be insulted, offended or shocked if people walked out during the dirty jokes. As he prophetically remarked, "Why should they enjoy watching Sonia take her clothes off when they've undressed in the dark since childhood? None of them have ever seen a naked woman's body, even the women."

Everyone was nervous. Some of the nervous people were grown-ups. Dr Hennessey, who played the part of the priest, went to the toilet about six times before his first appearance. Nicholas's hands were shaking so badly Sonia offered to dress him. I followed her into the men's changing room and found the rest of the male cast lined up in front of the mirrors, trousers round their ankles, plastering on make-up like in the ladies' toilet at a disco.

It was a shambles. Sonia removed her stocking provocatively and someone tut-tutted in the front row. It threw her so badly I had to leap into action as continuity person and help her out with a couple of sentences.

Afterwards she sucked on a cigarette (they were giving her mouth ulcers but she was determined to master them), and said, "Was that Reverend Robinson or Mrs Mulholland or your mother in the front row, Marian? God, it was terrifying. I went on stage and acted Heather the prostitute being Sonia Anderson. I could have been stripping in my bedroom all by myself. Forget the audience and Mr Stewart. I could hear myself saying all my lines and my voice sounded too loud. It was bizarre."

"At least you didn't stall," I said helpfully, "and when you mixed the sentences round it only made you sound more drunk."

Mr Stewart slapped her on the bum and said that, even with her breeding and her ashtray breath, she was still the best whore he'd ever taken to bed.

I had warmed to Mr Stewart's rather suspect charm. He was always charming no matter how badly things were going. I wished Jonathan could be so outwardly calm in the face of disaster. He'd phoned me about five in a panic. "Marian, I don't know if I can make it for eight, from Belfast, I've got a meeting now and there's fog on the motorway."

Hardly a life-and-death situation. "I'll meet you afterwards, then," I said in my new air stewardess voice, practising for when I would have to put nervous fliers at their ease. "There's a play post mortem at the rugby club at half ten, Jonathan."

So at least we know it wasn't Jonathan tut-tutting at Sonia in the front row.

Then there was a disturbance about beer glasses in Act Two. The dancers removed all the glasses from the dresser and Mr Stewart forgot his lines and Dr Hennessey refused to drink out of the only glass left on stage which had a crack in it. As Sonia said, "A true professional amateur would have drunk petrol out of the glass, had the part demanded it."

Then the fight got out of hand when one of the townie villains (we think it was Nicholas) actually did kick Mr Stewart in the head and Jimmy Fingers (playing the part of the One-Man Band) said, "Right, now, ladies and gentlemen, let's have no more of that nastiness," and started to play *The Birdie Song* on his electric organ. He was only excited because he'd heard that "wonderful, beautiful" Lynette was in the audience.

I had arranged to meet Jonathan in the rugby club at half ten but, for one reason and another, I was unavoidably delayed when the play finished. Standing guard while Sonia and Nicholas had another session behind the scenery, acting referee as Lynette criticised Jimmy's rendition of *Paper Roses* on the electric organ, and finally tearing Sonia off Lynette when Lynette revealed that it had been her tut-tutting in the front row during Sonia's strip.

"I did it for a laugh," said Lynette defiantly.

I was on my way to the rugby club when Mr Stewart

asked me to make a shopping list, "beer glasses and toilet rolls," for the following night.

"I think Marian should be voted 'man of the match' tonight," Mr Stewart announced, "since she said more on stage than the rest of us put together."

Anyway, I had no urge to leave the action and join Jonathan in the rugby club. He was Cecil in *A Room with a View*, I always pictured him indoors. I waited till Nicholas reappeared from behind the scenery and offered to walk up with him. Poor Nicholas.

"That Lynette," he said as we finally made our guilty way to the rugby club, hours late, "Sonia's sister. She has beautiful manners, hasn't she? But she'll have to come down to my level if I'm ever talking to her."

Tower of Strength Stephanie and Jonathan were sharing a table in the rugby club with Mandy Gorgon. They had faces on them like fur hatchets. I could see Jonathan was on the verge of calving yet another quilt with fringes. He stood up as I arrived.

"I'm just leaving, Marian," he said politely. "You can stay behind if you like. Maybe Sonia could give you a lift. Or Nicholas. Or whoever it was you preferred to spend the evening with."

We sat silently in the car on the way home. It was only another "much ado about nothing" row, I thought, it doesn't mean anything, he'll still love me tomorrow.

"Why are you huffing?" I asked eventually. "Was Mandy Gorgon no fun anymore?"

"I didn't drive from Belfast in the fog to meet Mandy Gorgon," he snapped. "I came a very long way in fog to see you, Marian, and I don't think it was really worth it."

Next morning I got the letter. The one I'd been waiting for. That told me I'd got the job as an air stewardess.

I had to read it twice because the first time my hands were shaking so badly I couldn't see beyond, "We are delighted . . ." They were delighted to inform me that I'd been selected for the Easter batch of new recruits. A six-week training course in London would commence on April the fifteenth. Classes would be taken in safety procedures, first aid and cabin services and grooming. Did I have any preferences about the country I'd like to be posted to after the training course? I could be posted anywhere in the world.

April the fifteenth. The day I was due to start in London was Easter Saturday, two days before I was due to get married.

For five whole minutes I felt like my mother feels when someone offers her the good news or the bad news first. I was six feet tall and floating but ready to be airsick on the way down.

"God," I told Him, for He was the only person I could share the news with, "God, I think I'm calving a quilt with fringes." I went to the doctor's clinic for my typhoid vaccination immediately. I was prepared to go anywhere in the world but "lovely" Goa or a Greek Island.

After she jabbed me, the nurse said it made most people pretty sick, but some died of brain problems. While we were waiting to discover if I was among the fatal minority, she asked me if I was going away anywhere "nice", (another adjective Miss French the English mistress would fail her students for using).

"I don't know yet," I said truthfully. "My fiancé has taken complete charge of our honeymoon destination."

Then I added, "He just said to pack for somewhere hot."

The injection made my arm ache, as if I'd been shot. All evening I nursed it as if it was broken and nobody appeared to notice at home. My mother believes sympathy encourages hypochondria. By teatime, however, I was convinced I was one of the fatal minority after all and I was dying.

"I can't eat," I said faintly. "I feel sick."

"It's anorexia," said my mother, "I knew you'd caught it, Marian. Your stomach has shrunk so small your mind tells you you can't swallow food. I'm telling you, Marian, that's what it is."

"Mummy," I said patiently, "I got a typhoid injection this afternoon. That means I'm suffering from typhoid as I sit here. That's why I'm shaking so much and my arm is hanging off and if I sniff food I want to throw up. It has nothing to do with my diet."

"I wasn't a bit sick when I got that jab last summer," she said firmly. "It's not like you to overreact about anything, dear."

"Your jab was for tetanus," I said, "tetanus doesn't make you sick."

What did I have to do to convince her? Die of brain problems? Stephen suddenly woke from his reverie at the end of the table.

"What did you get a typhoid injection for, Marian?" he said.

"Well, I still don't know where Jonathan and I are going on honeymoon," I said, mopping my pale face with the dishcloth. "I didn't like to ask Jonathan when it's the groom's prerogative but I've dropped enough hints about the Caribbean, and I'm sure you need loads of jabs before you go there."

"Why do you want to go to the Caribbean?" asked my mother. Only my mother could wonder why someone wanted to go to the Caribbean.

"Well, there are big resorts with piles of things to do," I said patiently in my air stewardess voice. "And the price is all-inclusive so Jonathan won't have to worry about daily budgets and the allocation of my pocket money."

"It sounds like a waste of money to me," she said pessimistically, "going away somewhere like that when you'll only have one thing on your mind. In my day, couples went on honeymoon to get to know each other better. Your father and I spent two days by the lakes in Fermanagh."

I laughed. My poor fat little mother. If she hadn't been so grotesquely excited about my wedding, maybe I could have confided in her about the air stewardess job and jilting Jonathan. And she could have assured me that my major doubts about getting married were only wedding jitters and anybody with half a brain caught them and usually it foretold a blissful marriage. She might have even managed to persuade me that the solution to wedding jitters was not necessarily the supreme sacrifice. "Stop the world, I want to get off."

"I think I'd check with Jonathan about your honeymoon destination," said my mother, "in case you're getting injections and missing meals unnecessarily. If you get any thinner, Marian, my wedding dress will be hanging off you."

So, after the final night performance party, I phoned Jonathan and said, "All right, Jonathan, the play is over and I'm ready to talk weddings. Have you been inoculated yet?"

"What for, Marian?"

"For our honeymoon, darling," I said firmly. "It's always best to get them well before the wedding in case there's an allergic reaction or something and we swell up."

"I shouldn't think we'll need inoculations," said Jonathan calmly.

"Have you got it organised, then?" I said. "Don't tell me where it is, Jonathan. Excite me. Just tell me to pack for somewhere hot."

Jonathan said nothing for a moment. There was a pregnant pause, then he said, "Don't be silly, Marian, we aren't going foreign at Easter. We can't. Not with house prices the way they are. I don't think we can even afford a stand-by to Greece this year. Maybe for a week in the autumn, if we're lucky."

"So where are we going, Jonathan?" I said woodenly. I had the "Bad News" feeling, the airsick one.

"Since you ask, I've got us a bungalow in Donegal for Easter week. Nicholas Stewart offered it as a wedding present. I think that was jolly decent of him when we hardly know each other. I think it will be very romantic, myself." I put down the phone and I took my engagement ring off and decided not to wear it ever again.

I went downstairs to tell my mother that it was all off. He wouldn't buy me a Byzantine wedding ring. He planned to take me to Donegal on honeymoon. I was calling the wedding off.

"Marian," she said, "Marian, why aren't you wearing your engagement ring? Have you lost it, Marian? I told you it would slip off your finger now you've got so thin. Oh Marian, you can be so careless sometimes. I told you to take it to the jewellers to have it tightened."

I sighed. I'd been waiting twenty-eight years to hear a word of spontaneous sympathy from her. Why change the habits of a lifetime?

"Well, I've taken your advice, Mummy," I said. "The ring is at the jewellers but it won't be ready until Easter Saturday, the man says."

"Just in time for the wedding," she said, relieved.

"And I took your advice about checking the honeymoon destination with Jonathan," I added calmly. "And you were right again. We aren't going foreign at Easter, we're going to Donegal. So if you're making chips this evening, I'll be delighted to eat a plate of them for you."

"Donegal?" she repeated. Even she was shocked. Her harmless fantasies about my wedding might never have included a Caribbean honeymoon, but anyone could see she hadn't prepared herself for Donegal either.

She rallied well. My mother has had twenty-eight

years of rallying well. "We'll just tell everyone that it's a secret," she suggested. "We'll tell them all that Jonathan said was to pack for somewhere hot. No one will ever ask to see the honeymoon photographs."

"Or we could just tell everyone that we stayed in bed the whole time and didn't take any."

She smiled at me.

"You're taking this very well, Marian," she said.

"So are you, Mummy."

Determined to have the last word, trying to be kind, she said, "You have great childbearing hips for an anorexic, Marian."

chapter twenty

Lynette was at one side of a mountain and she wanted to be at the other side. But, short of blowing up the bloody mountain, how was she going to get to the other side?

She had been offered a "broadcasting opportunity" in Belfast. Head of Radio Programmes phoned her and asked her if she was interested in broadcasting, they thought she might be amusing "on air".

"I have a low boredom threshold," said Lynette, "I'm interested in everything. And within a week she'd packed her bags and taken the train from Dublin.

I met her at the train station. Once upon a time, when sisters were devoted to each other, Sonia would have made a point of dropping all, and meeting her in Nicholas's black BMW with the personalised number plates. But Sonia was busy. She was getting her perm cut out in the morning, she was having a facial in the afternoon, Nicholas and she had a dinner party in the evening.

"NO."

"What has made me like this?" asked Sonia, laughing, "Nicholas and I make a lot of noise together."

"I don't know the first thing about broadcasting," said Lynette. "But I do know that people love to talk about men, women, sex and scandal. Exhaustively."

Lynette considered herself a "creative person", someone "too scatty to earn a decent wage", an "artist". But she was a very arrogant artist, not an insecure one. (As Jimmy Fingers found to his cost.) She was far too clever and ambitious to tie herself to anything for long. Had she been a security addict like me, she would have taken the three-book contract and colossal advance offered her by an English publishing house at twenty-one. Three-book contracts are the civil service of creative writing says Lynette.

"With a three-book contract," Lynette explained, "I could have got engaged to Jimmy after university and married to him after teacher training, and had a couple of package holidays with him to Cyprus before giving birth to little Fingers." She sighed.

"That was a big sigh, Lynette," I said mildly.

"Gerry and I aren't interested in a twenty-four-hour relationship with each other any more," said Lynette. "I worked hard so it would never happen, but we'd started to become a normal couple. We were shopping together on Saturday and going for drives on Sunday. He'd started to scold me for lying about that flat all day scribbling in my pyjamas. I've just escaped in time, you know. I saw a holiday brochure in the hall cupboard."

"Opened at the Greek islands?"

214

The same week Jimmy Fingers applied to be an announcer at the BBC. It was advertised in the *Belfast Telegraph*, to cover a period of maternity leave.

The announcer wouldn't actually appear on the screen so the fact that Jimmy looked somewhat eccentric in the flesh didn't matter. All the announcer needed was a cool head and a nice voice. I've said before that Jimmy was born with better talent than looks. Jimmy's voice could charm the birds out of the trees. And the knickers off you. So, provided Lynette wasn't in the same room as him, when his temperature rose and his voice became falsetto with nerves, Jimmy was the ideal candidate.

Jimmy graduated from Queen's with a degree in biology and a mobile karaoke machine he'd won one night with his rendition of *Never Felt More Like Singing the Blues*. Winning had been his destruction. Destined for stardom, he refused to take a proper job. Onward and upward he went, to amateur dramatics, Young Farmer public speaking competitions, solo guitar at church parties.

He had been slogging half-heartedly at a PhD in biochemistry for four years. Scraping the white blood cells of artificial kidneys. Working the petrol pumps of his uncle's garage at the weekends. Official photographer at weddings, funerals and *barmitzvahs*. Dreaming of fame and fortune in a world without artificial kidneys. It was only time before opportunity knocked.

"What did I ever see in such a loser?" asked Lynette.

He was on the fringe of everything, belonging nowhere, unhappy, discontent, dissatisfied, with ants in his ambitious pants. Afraid to stop hovering in case he got stuck in life's sticky tape. He was a lot more like Lynette than you could imagine.

I went up to the old studio that smelled of cat pee to book him for my wedding. Little had changed. Most of the equipment still wasn't paid for. Jimmy dug out the photographs of my "interesting" face that he'd taken for the *Elle* talent competition, and we laughed at them.

"I'm sorry you didn't win," I said.

He shook his head, pointing to a newly-framed photograph of Lynette on the wall beside his A level photography certificate.

"That was my greatest moment," he said.

Lynette had signed the photograph. "Was this your fifteen minutes of fame, Jimmy?"

When Lynette heard that Jimmy had been short-listed for the announcers job, she popped round to the garage and insisted he give her a guided tour of the fresh meats counter. Then she bought a fizzy lollipop and he checked her car for oil and fixed the dodgy windscreen wiper with the pin of the golliwog brooch he gave her when they started going steady.

"That strange creature claims to be content with his life," Lynette mused. "Isn't he an awful liar? He looks terrible, worse than usual. Big hollow eyes and stubble on his pale face. He thinks he has finally placed me in a box you know, with a lid on it, and 'Lynette Anderson RIP' on the outside. I think maybe I'll just start calling round to the garage more often, popping up unexpected and causing trouble."

"So his interview is this afternoon," I said.

"Yes, and he's asked me to keep my fingers crossed and you have to pray for him that he gets the job," she said, looking at the clock. "Maybe I'll just phone him and ask him how it went."

"And if he's got it," I suggested, "you could buy him dinner to celebrate. Not that I'm trying to matchmake or anything."

"Never chase a man," said Lynette, "they can smell desperation." And she sprinted into the hall and rang his house. Lynette has an astonishing memory. She didn't even have to look the number up.

The phone rang once. "This is foolish," squeaked Lynette. "Why doesn't he have an answering machine so I can leave a message?"

"The Golden Rules say you can let it ring five times," I reminded her, and on the fifth ring Jimmy lifted it.

Sometimes I wondered about Jimmy. What could Lynette see in someone, I was almost going to say a "man", who jilted her because he claimed she wasn't the girl he fell in love with. He once told me in a drunken and nostalgic moment that he was afraid to phone her.

He was always like that, of course. Jimmy Fingers gave a breezy air of confidence but he was really quite backward beneath it all. There was apprehension in his eyes.

Jimmy said, "So you'll be in Belfast all alone for the weekend, Lynette."

"I'm not phoning you so you'll ask me out for the weekend," said Lynette haughtily. "I'm phoning to offer

217

to buy you dinner, to celebrate your new job and the fact we're now colleagues. You don't have to accept if you don't want to."

It was a date.

"If he thinks he can waltz back into my knickers with that velvet-smooth voice of his, he can think again," she said defiantly when she saw me smirking. "Jimmy only ever loved me in tight jeans and a big smile. I'm not going to be nicey-nicey to him just in case he might fall in love with me again. He didn't love me the last time. And I'm not going to waste my charmed and wonderful talents worrying about why he jilted me then."

"Lynette," I said firmly, "you only phoned to offer him dinner, to celebrate the fact he has finally got a job and some self-respect. And, unless I've missed the subtext of the conversation, he only accepted. He probably wants you to give out the prizes at the Young Farmers' dinner dance. Or maybe he wants to ask about the personal fall-out of fame . . . You know, how it can fester for years between couples who used to love each other . . ."

There is no denying that fame brings its own set of rules. People think your emotions automatically become public property so no one ever treats you exactly the same ever again. Lynette had been approached by old schoolfriends who said, "I saw you on the *Kelly Show* and you were really immense," or, "You were really lucky, weren't you?"

Some of them tried to charm her into bed so they could boast about it afterwards. She said Johnboy Jackson told her that he'd beat her about the head with a ruler in third year biology because he fancied her. And Jimmy Fingers, plonker that he was, dumped her because he couldn't compete.

"I don't want to give out prizes at the Young Farmers' dinner dance," said Lynette hysterically. "And I'm not going to lecture Jimmy on the price of success in case it frightens him off and he starts scraping kidneys again and selling petrol."

"Lynette," I said crossly, "you and Jimmy are suffering a classic seven-year itch. It's seven years since you were plucked from obscurity and made a star. And you still haven't resolved your relationship with Jimmy."

Lynette had met her Waterloo and she was determined that I was going to share every bit of it. She phoned me at seven the morning of the date.

"I dreamt you and Jimmy got married, Marian," she said. "You looked wonderful in a white hat with net on it. I was devastated and wanted to go straight home. I kept running away from both of you and you kept laughing at me. And then I dreamt that I had my A level biology exam and I'd not studied for it. I frequently have that dream about the biology exam. I'm frantically trying to remember what month it is and what time the exam starts, and what day and what subjects on the course I have to study and it wakes me up. It often takes a minute before I remember that it's only a dream."

"Lynette," I said, "try to remember that he's going to be just as nervous as you."

It might be coldness on my part, but I don't like to get too close to anyone (emotionally or physically). I don't like people telling me their problems and I don't tell anyone mine. That's why I never told when the Gorgons bullied me at school. Why I never asked Sonia about the details of Neil's death. Fundamentally I am a cold and unaffectionate person. It's not fear of rejection makes me like this, nor, as I used to think, is it a pathological desire to sweep things under the carpet. And it's nothing to do with my mother. I might have been unfortunate with the one I was allocated but she is no worse or no better than anyone else's. It's too easy to place all the blame for my inadequacies on her. Mrs Lamb and Mrs Anderson would have been just as bad. And imagine if Mandy Gorgon was my mother?

I was born seeing things objectively. I'm the splash of cold water in life, the slap on the face of hysteria.

So my heart sank when Lynette appeared on my doorstep weeping piteously.

"I suppose I was expecting a miracle and I'm crying because I didn't get one," she said.

Everything had gone well on the surface. They dined and wined and screwed and giggled and drank a bottle of wine and were snuggled up in bed all lovey-dovey and like someone with an addiction or an itch that couldn't be scratched, she asked him if he ever missed her.

Poor Jimmy. What the hell did that mean?

Jimmy had had a rough night at the Young Farmers' club prize-giving and dinner dance. When he blurted out to Johnboy Jackson that Lynette was buying him dinner, Johnboy laughed maniacally over his pint.

"Are you still jumping when that slag clicks her

fingers?" he said, "She sat beside me in biology at school and she was mad for it even then. Did no one tell you she sleeps around, Jimmy?"

Maybe not. No one had told him that Johnboy Jackson was a rejected seducer. Jimmy Fingers did the only violent and macho thing he'd ever done in his life.

He rugby-tackled Johnboy to the floor and sat on his face till he apologised (the band were playing *Never Felt More Like Singing the Blues*, appropriately).

"Your head's soft," said Johnboy who thought the whole thing was hysterically funny.

I don't know who was more surprised, Johnboy or Jimmy.

"No, Lynette," said Jimmy. "It took three years to get over my broken heart completely and I was horribly confused and unhappy for a long time. But now I've found my feet. I'm a happy man."

"So what are you doing in bed with me?" asked Lynette. Jimmy shrugged. "I don't rightly know, Lynette," he said. "I fancied you better when your ears stuck out and your tits were smaller. I liked your hair when it was mousy brown."

"You used to have manners," said Lynette, "it was the only thing you ever had going for you. You couldn't even kiss." And all night they tore each other apart, saying nastier and nastier things, lying rigidly side by side, neither wanting to get out of bed and leave the other forever. Letting all the wonderful dreams they'd been saving for "Happy Ever After" evaporate like dust around them.

"And I've never felt more unloved and wretched and sad in my life," Lynette said. "It's very empty at the top when you have no one to share it with."

"But you know what Jimmy Fingers is like," I said callously. "Once a frog, always a frog. Did you expect him to turn into a handsome prince just because you kissed him?"

"When Jimmy loved me he phoned and visited every night of the week," said Lynette. "He was crazy about me and it was fun even when we fought. I loved eating fish and chips and snogging in the pictures and wearing blue jeans and a big smile. One night in bed before I left him, I rolled into Gerry and stroked his hand the way I used to stroke Jimmy's and then I rolled back and woke up. Or maybe I dreamt the whole thing."

"Lynette," I said, "you could have any man you want."

"But I don't want anyone else," she wailed.

"My Aunt Angela says that not all men are handsome princes, and not all women are damsels in distress," I said. "With equality and all that you could ride up and save Jimmy if you wanted to."

So Lynette put on a pair of jeans, bought a huge bottle of wine and stopped for a chicken vindaloo takeaway on the way to Jimmy's cottage. She was quaking with fear, she said. If he had visitors, she would turn the car and drive straight back home again.

Jimmy opened the back door, burst into tears, snogged the life out of her and said, "I really, really love you."

chapter twenty-one

"Cheer up, Marian," said Sonia, "it's supposed to be your hen party. You're meant to get drunk and enjoy yourself. Blow up one of these strawberry-flavoured condoms and put it on your head."

"Don't tease, Sonia," I said wearily, "I've had more than enough to drink. I can't hold it any more now that I'm nine stones."

"Well, it's time you practiced a bit more," she said offering me her straw, which had a pink plastic penis attached to it. "It'll take more than strong drink to keep you married to Jonathan."

"Stop it, Sonia," I said. "I'm doubtful enough as it is." She thought I was joking. She put her arm around me and burped gin and tonic into my face.

"It's only wedding jitters, Marian," she said solemnly. "Everyone with half a brain catches them. They foretell a blissful marriage. And, before you ask, no, I never felt any before I married Paddy Butler."

Manic laughter.

Lynette had a strawberry-flavoured condom on her head. "Would you come on my show, Marian," she said, "the morning of your wedding and talk about wedding jitters? We could have a phone-in."

More manic laughter.

All week I'd been packing. When I left Magherafelt, I was taking my life with me. Twenty-eight years crammed into the suitcase set Stephen bought me as a wedding present. It was like one of those stupid psychological tests Jonathan used to do on us when he was at Queen's. "If your house was on fire and there was only one thing you could rescue, what would it be?" (Creative and all as she claimed to be, Lynette had promptly said, "The receipt of my insurance policy".)

It's incredible what junk accumulates in twenty-eight years. I knew I was never coming back to Magherafelt and that made selection harder. I was slipping unnoticed out of my old life. When I got on the plane in Aldergrove I would be as one dead. To quote Jonathan, I was making my bed and I was going to lie in it forever.

It would be a work of necessity, not an act of self-indulgence, to reinvent myself beyond recognition. I used to imagine this metamorphosis would occur at university when I would live in a bed-sit and wear bright-coloured painter's overalls and be very small and thin. Extravagant fantasies, which didn't involve Jonathan either. The vision comforted me through the drag of my A levels, and the tedium of teacher training. I kept waiting for it to happen, never once actively looking for escape. I was a whingeing child who blamed my mother, my environment and my unattractiveness for my fatalism.

But now I was getting a second chance.

I really didn't feel I was missing out by not having someone to share the excitement with. When I was lying in bed, unable to sleep, and my mother was cheerfully reassuring me that it was wedding nerves, I often imagined how she would react. She would have been in her element as a prophetess of doom.

"You'll never stick the work, Marian, you're so lazy. And I've been told that the majority of air stewardesses are drug addicts trying to cope with jet lag."

And if I was posted to New York after the training?

"You'll be raped and murdered living there, Marian, country bumpkin, wet behind the ears."

And if I was sent to the Middle East?

"You'll get your hands chopped off if you expose more that the point of your nose."

Sonia and Lynette would have thought it was mega. I would find myself an oil sheikh multimillionaire and he'd send his private jet to land in our church carpark to pick them up and bring them over for holidays. Maybe he'd marry all three of us, either one at a time or all three together.

Sonia and Lynette and my mother had always taken me passenger in their canoes. I'd paddled my own.

I kept waiting for my Christian Conscience, what was left of it, to speak up. To tell me that it was a dirty low stunt I was pulling. Had I no loyalty? Didn't I know that I was going to break my mother's heart? Jonathan would doubtless recover but the scandal and the shame would follow her to her grave. Had I no gratitude for the sacrifices she'd made for me? She had been trying so hard all week to be normal.

"Marian, pet," she said in the middle of the packing, "you're only going to Donegal."

"Perhaps," I said, folding a flannelette sheet, "but I'm also leaving home forever."

She had the decency to squeeze out a couple of maternal tears. "It's not like you're going to the other side of the world," she said. "You can come back and visit me at any time." I didn't see Jonathan, my fiancé who I was supposed to be marrying on Monday, until Easter Sunday afternoon. The sky didn't go black and hail didn't fall at three o'clock on Good Friday.

I hadn't given him much thought, really. He was probably baking buns and making visitors cups of tea at his house and thanking them for their wedding presents as I was doing. Jonathan was a handsome prince with middle-aged women. In fact everybody loved Jonathan, even me. But I wasn't in love with him. And that's what made all the difference.

He looked very serious when he saw me and the five suitcases. He didn't kiss me. Maybe there was something fundamentally dodgy about our relationship when we had no thought or desire to kiss or touch each other. I knew Lynette and Sonia weren't normal role models for anyone, but love, lust and sex are tactile and physical things for the both of them. They can't take their hands off the two boys. Stroking the inside of the leg and enquiring, "Are you all right pet?" is all in a normal night's shopping. Neither of the boys looking like they're going to freak.

Jonathan was like a sticking-plaster with an erection when we started going out together. But we'd been at first base in our relationship since the night that I finished my A level mocks and he suddenly went asexual on me.

"If we play with fire," he'd said, "we have to expect to get burnt."

Jonathan said, "I want to have a very serious talk with you, Marian. Can I take you out for a drink?"

I laughed nervously. "Take me to Kate's," I said, "the pub for underage drinkers. Some of my fourth year English class can buy us the drinks."

There was no way in the world that he'd found out I was running away to be an air stewardess.

I'd bought my ticket to London under an assumed name and paid for it with cash (and I wore a headscarf and dark glasses in the travel agents).

"I confess," I said lightly when we were settled in Kate's. "I asked Mrs Mulholland to play *Here Comes The Bride* instead of the Bridal March from *Lohengrin* by Wagner. It was my mother's idea. 'Here Comes The Bride, short, fat and wide, slipped on a piece of glass and fell on her ass.' Have you never heard that rhyme, Jonathan?"

Jonathan told me something psychological once about men and a Madonna Whore complex. He said the male's perception of the female is either black or white. Men don't have grey areas in their minds. To Jonathan, I'm a

Madonna figure, not as in the singer of *Papa Don't Preach*, but Madonna as in the Mother of God. Above the natural urges of life. A pure person. I had always assumed that was why he stopped trying to seduce me years before. And why he got so cross when I talked dirty.

"I'm not here to talk about wedding music," said Jonathan, "or honeymoon destinations. I know you wanted to go to the Caribbean, Marian, and I'm sorry. I appreciate that girls dream about weddings all their lives. But, Marian, we aren't young fools wearing rose-coloured glasses. If we're going to be man and wife we have to be honest with each other."

"If?" I interrupted, surprised. "Do you not want to marry me, Jonathan?"

"That's not what I'm saying, Marian. What I'm saying is that I think we should have thrown caution to the winds and married when we were twenty," said Jonathan miserably. "I never thought a relationship could pass its sell-by date. I thought that when two people were committed to each other it didn't matter how long it took to get to the wedding. You and I have been going backwards instead of forwards for nearly ten years, Marian. I think we've been flogging a dead horse and raking over the ashes for too long. Our relationship has never passed first base."

"What are you saying?" I asked. I didn't understand. "Is there something worrying you? Something you want to tell me? Do you have a guilty conscience about something, Jonathan?"

Was he telling me he didn't want to marry me?

Jonathan sighed. "Mandy Gorgon's daughter is mine," he said. "I'm sorry."

Mandy Gorgon? I'm sorry? For a minute I couldn't even remember who Mandy Gorgon was.

"Mandy Gorgon, the hairdresser?" I let a big shout out of me. I hadn't meant to, it just slipped out, but Jonathan dropped his glass of orange juice with shock. He blushed and started blustering.

"Jonathan," I said, "can I give you a word of advice since we're being honest with each other? When you drop a drink you should say, 'Fuck that, get me another'."

"Yes, Marian, Mandy Gorgon. She was in your class at school. Her daughter, my daughter, is in your English class."

"But she's the most foul-mouthed child I have," I said. "She can't say 'Please, Miss' without swearing in the middle of it."

"Marian, Mandy slept with every boy in Magherafelt the year of her A levels, she was a very obliging girl, and maybe she doesn't know who the father of her baby is herself. But her daughter is the image of my mother."

"So that's why you stopped trying to seduce me," I said. "Why you've been asexual with me for ten years. Sonia said you were religious or impotent or gay."

"Please listen to me, Marian. You were studying for your A levels. I'd come and visit and we'd kiss on the sofa and, if I was lucky, I got touching your breasts on the outside of your jumper and then your mother would bang the living-room door and you would say, 'No, Jonathan.' And ram a pile of religion down my throat and I'd have to go home."

"So it was my fault?" I said, "that you got Mandy Gorgon pregnant? Because I was a Miss Garden Path? Why could you not have done a few more sit-ups like every other sexually frustrated teenager in the world? Why could you not have bought a packet of condoms?"

No wonder Mandy Gorgon had been so nice to me during our A levels. I knew she was up to something. That slippy bitch. Jonathan wasn't much of a possession, but he had belonged to me. Mandy Gorgon hated Sonia and me as much as we hated her. The only thing she could do better than us was the one thing we didn't try at school. My mother once told me she was the bicycle of Magherafelt. Poor Mummy.

"Listen to me, Marian. I was being driven mad with frustration. The night of Neil Anderson's christening party, I wanted us to make love. I said so. Upstairs in Anderson's house. Do you remember?"

Of course I remembered. That was the night I drank two glasses of wine and thought I was an alcoholic.

"Mandy Gorgon wasn't at the party," I said. "Sonia and I didn't associate with sluts when we were at school."

"Weren't you even curious, Marian?"

"Only in a biological sense," I said truthfully. "I took you to Betty Blue when it was on at the pictures, didn't I? You were the one who was disgusted, not me."

"But you never wanted to know what a real man looked like," said Jonathan.

That was because the man I loved didn't want me.

What a strange thought to slip unbidden into my head.

"There is a time and a place for everything," I said crossly, "the middle of my A level preparations, aged seventeen, was hardly the time or the place."

The man I wanted was a fantasy man. A knight in shining armour. A rugby boy who was a sensitive type. A man who would let me make the decisions but sweep me off my feet at the same time. He wasn't a living breathing man who made mistakes.

"I wanted desperately to tell you about Mandy," said Jonathan. "After your mock A levels I took you out to dinner to *The Rainbow's End*. I was going to tell you that night. But you told me you'd two-timed me at Jimmy Fingers's charity disco. I thought you were going to finish with me. So I didn't tell you. It sounded too much like tit for tat."

"You were late but I didn't turn up?" I said. It's a Golden Rule if you've been stood up. To say, "Were you late, darling? I didn't turn up."

"I don't understand," said Jonathan.

"Jimmy Fingers's charity disco," I said. "I didn't two-time you at it. I didn't even go."

"Yes, you did. You said you faced some strange boy who was there, you didn't know his name."

I really hadn't gone to Jimmy Fingers's charity disco. I'd worked at *The Rainbow's End* that night. At a rugby Old Boys' dinner dance. So many rugby-playing bums together. Talking about setting up tries and kicking ass. Some of the boys were in Neil Anderson's class at school. They threw his name about in the conversation with a familiarity that sickened me. "He must be dead three or four years," said one. "It was the year we did our A levels. Do you remember his sister, Sonia? She was in fourth year at the time. She had big bushy eyebrows and a fat friend. They say she was in the Mental after it."

"I was in the car that night," said another. "His brains were smashed all over the windscreen."

My head was swimming, the words almost choking me. I set a round of drinks on the table and dashed to the toilets to be sick. Lovely smiling Neil, who called me a "little mouse", who made my glasses steam up with excitement. Marian "Oh so serious" French, the girl destined to die a virgin, the strait-laced goody, goody, the security addict, had melted away that day on the bus when he noticed me. And that fantasy about us at the disco just grew out of nowhere.

Every rugby boy fantasy I'd ever had, the hero was Neil Anderson. My knight in a shining rugby shirt. Except I used to call him Paddy Butler for the sake of argument. There was a logical reason for it. I read Wuthering Heights from cover to cover when I was doing my English A level. Look at the fool Heathcliff made of himself when Cathy died. So I used Paddy Butler for the sake of argument. Except for the night of Jimmy Fingers's charity disco. And that was so good I almost believed it myself.

"It doesn't matter now," I said, "Whether I went to Jimmy Fingers's disco or not. It's too late for all that now. But Mandy Gorgon, Jonathan. What strange taste in women you have, darling."

"It's never too late to back out," said Jonathan

nervously, "and it'll be a damned sight cheaper now than after the wedding."

I smiled at Jonathan. There is one Golden Rule that I've never used because I never knew what it meant. "Always be true to yourself." My mother wrote it once on the inside of an autograph book.

Now I know that sometimes the only way to ride up and save someone is to let them go.

"What are you doing tomorrow morning?" I smiled. "I need a lift to the airport."

Also published by Poolbeg

The Pineapple Tart

by

Anne Dunlop

Helen Gordon, the narrator of this novel, is the pineapple tart, "the highest form of compliment any woman can be given." Helen has four sisters, three of whom attend the same university as she. The Gordon sisters have escaped from an eccentric household in Northern Ireland and use their stay in Dublin as an opportunity for "shifting" men by the dozen. Their story is full of excitement, disaster and romance.

Not since Enda O'Brien's *The Country Girls* have experiences of a wild but essentially innocent girlhood been so effectively and elegantly captured. Readers will be charmed to make the acquaintance of the gorgeous Helen Gordon and her sisters.

ISBN 1-85371-405-4

Also published by Poolbeg

A Soft Touch

by

Anne Dunlop

The gorgeous Helen Gordon is back and so are the rest of her eccentric family (all except Jennifer who after a shotgun wedding lives in the wilds of Kerry with a family of vets).

Life in Derryrose is as chaotic as ever: Daisy has changed from airhead to farmer; Laura has left her American husband for good and her twin babies, Shaun and Scarlett, rule the roost; Sarah the teacher has turned feminist; and Helen, the original pineapple tart, still has not found the love of her life.

Those who read *The Pineapple Tart*, Anne Dunlop's sparkling first novel, will renew old friendships. New readers will be delighted to make the acquaintance of this remarkable family.

ISBN 1-85371-404-6

Also published by Poolbeg

The Dolly Holiday

by

Anne Dunlop

The wickedly funny voice of Helen Gordon, heroine of *The Pineapple Tart* and *A Soft Touch*, is heard again in this beguiling sequel to the Derryrose saga.

Helen has got herself a job as Assistant to an Assistant in the Wild West Theme Park. Despite her intention to claw and grovel her way to the top, her abnormally high interest in members of the opposite sex and her infatuation with her best friend's bridegroom distract her.

In *The Dolly Holiday*, Helen is a young woman who has fallen out of love with love but who still yearns for romantic make-believe.

ISBN 1-85371-325-2